DATE DUE

JUST FOR FINS

Don't miss all the fin-flicking romance:

FORGIVE MY FINS
FINS ARE FOREVER

TERA LYNN CHILDS

Fins #3

JUST FOR FINS

MCPL-HM

3 2611 050709720

KATHERINE TEGEN BOOKS
An Imprint of HarperCollins Publishers

Katherine Tegen Books is an imprint of HarperCollins Publishers.

Just for Fins
Printed in the United States of America.
www.epicreads.com

Library of Congress Cataloging-in-Publication Data
Childs, Tera Lynn.
   Just for fins / by Tera Lynn Childs. — 1st ed.
     p.   cm.
   Summary: "As the mermaid Crown Princess of Thalassinia, Lily must dive
deep into finding a solution when she discovers the ocean's warming is causing
big waves for both mermaids and humans"— Provided by publisher.
   ISBN 978-0-06-219215-8 (hardback)
   [1. Mermaids—Fiction. 2. Princesses—Fiction. 3. Global warming—Fiction.
4. Environmental disasters—Fiction.] I. Title.
PZ7.C44185 Jus 2012   2011052404
[Fic]—dc23   CIP
                                                                  AC

Typography by Andrea Vandergrift
12 13 14 15 16   LP/RRDH   10 9 8 7 6 5 4 3 2 1
❖
First Edition

For my Daddy
words aren't enough
but they'll have to do
Donald J. Childs
1943–2011

"*H*ow can you not know how to use the royal seal?"

I glare at Dosinia across the kitchen table. She looks fashionably bored as always, her perfectly glossed mouth pursed out in a disapproving pucker. If there weren't stacks of kelpaper and pots of waterproof squid ink between us, I'd be tempted to jump over the table to throttle her.

Besides, with Brody practically glued to her side—as close as Aunt Rachel's wooden chairs will allow—he'd get equally doused with the thick liquid. And I'm sure Prithi, the furry little traitor, is curled around her feet. They're innocent bystanders in this family squabble.

So instead of lashing out, I grumble, "I *do*. I'm just out of practice."

Of course, I'm not so sure I know what I'm doing. I've never sent out invitations to a council of kings and queens before. I've never even sent out any sort of invitation other than to birthday parties, and those usually had bubbles and seahorses on them, not royal seals. This is a level of responsibility I've never faced.

I need to get used to it.

As of my eighteenth birthday two days ago, I am officially Crown Princess of Thalassinia, which means all my correspondence—my underwater correspondence, anyway—has to bear my royal seal. It looks just like Daddy's, except that instead of saying KING WHELK OF THALASSINIA, it says CROWN PRINCESS WATERLILY.

Every time I stamp the seal onto a sheet of kelpaper, I smile with pride. And to think I almost gave all this up. I glance sideways up at Quince and find him sniffing the open pot of dark-blue squid ink. I bite back a laugh when he jerks away at the disgusting smell.

He must sense my attention, because he looks over at me. His expression shifts from scowl to sultry in a fin flick when he finds me watching him. He winks at me, and I feel my cheeks burn hot with a blush. If we weren't surrounded by friends and family right now, he'd probably be saying, "Like what you see, princess?"

Oh yeah, he would have been worth the sacrifice, for sure. But I'm glad I found a way to keep both him *and* my title.

"On an official state invitation like this," Dosinia says, interrupting my moment with Quince, "your seal should be placed at the *bottom* of the correspondence. Not the top."

"You——" I start to argue with her, but then a long-forgotten lesson from the royal tutor resurfaces. Before I came to live on land with Aunt Rachel, I had hours and hours of training in royal protocol. How to enter a dining room. What to wear to a state funeral. And, as much as it pains me to remember, where to place the royal seal on official correspondence.

That doesn't mean I like admitting that Doe is right. I *never* like admitting that.

Rather than give her the satisfaction—and the chance to say I told you so—I slump my shoulders, grab the stack of misstamped kelpaper, and drop it on the floor behind me.

"Is it that big a deal?" Shannen asks.

She's my best human friend, a certified genius, and always ready to lend a helping hand when I need something— anything—but she's not at all up to speed on mer-world etiquette. She doesn't know that a misplaced seal could mean the difference between an invitation being placed on a ruler's desk or tossed into the nearest trash bowl.

"Yeah," I say with a resigned sigh. "It kind of is."

Across the table, Doe sits up straighter. I can practically hear the gloating already. I keep my eyes on the table, pulling over another stack of kelpaper to start the whole stamping process over, and ignoring my cousin. If she doesn't want a bottle of squid ink sent flying her way, she'll keep her little bubble of pride to herself.

"See, I told you I could help," she says. "I had just as many hours of protocol training as you did. More since you left."

Prithi meows in agreement.

I slowly slide my hand across the table toward the foul-smelling dark-blue squid ink.

Brody doesn't release Doe's hand as he scoots his chair a few inches away from the line of fire.

"Who wants lemonade?" Aunt Rachel pushes back from the table. "Everyone? Lily?"

As everyone else says yes, I look up at her pointed use of my name to find her giving me an equally pointed look. Below raised brows, her wide-eyed gaze flashes to the pot of squid ink in my hand and back to my eyes. Busted.

I release the pot. "Yes," I say, dropping my eyes to my now-empty hands, "I'd love some."

"Excellent."

I stare at my fingers, covered in smudges of squid ink like when I was a little guppy just learning how to use sea-cucumber quills to write on kelpaper scrolls. Normally I would just use a prefilled pen, but official correspondence requires a more formal calligraphy.

Still, if my splotch-covered fingers are any indication, maybe someone should change that law.

"Relax, princess," Quince says, reaching over my hands to grab the stack of kelpaper and the royal seal. "Shannen and I can do the stamping. You focus on the writing."

I give him a grateful smile. "That would be great," I say. I point to a spot in the center of the bottom of the kelpaper sheet. "The seal should be stamped right there."

Shannen nods. "Got it."

She takes the squid-ink-doused sponge, presses the seal into it with a *squish*, and then carefully stamps the mark into the exact spot I indicated. Shannen is the neatest person I know. If anyone can make precision stamps on kelpaper, it's her.

Aunt Rachel returns to the table with a tray of lemonade-filled glasses. She sets one in front of each of us, careful to keep them away from the kelpaper.

I lift my glass to take a sip, waiting for the freshly stamped royal seal to dry so I can start composing the invitation without smearing the ink.

When Tellin and I talked on my birthday—both before and after the bond-in-name-only that allowed me to keep my crown and stay with Quince—we decided that calling a council of kings and queens was the best way to help his dying kingdom.

Ocean warming and coral bleaching are having catastrophic effects on Acropora. Things are so bad, Tellin almost forced me to bond with him because he thought a stronger alliance with Thalassinia would save them. When he explained what was going on, I couldn't swim away. I bonded with him, to retain my title and my power to call a council of kings and queens to make a formal request for aid.

For too long his father's pride kept them from asking for help. We have to act quickly now.

After my birthday ball, Tellin returned to his kingdom to share the news with his girlfriend and to prepare. He'll meet me back in Thalassinia this weekend for the council meeting. If everything goes according to plan, by the time the meeting is over, Acropora will have offers of supplies and support from every ruler in attendance.

With the seal dry on the first sheet of kelpaper, I stare down at the pale-blue expanse and nerves kick in. I know this is what needs to be done, and that my responsibilities as crown princess will only continue to grow. But still, the idea that I am writing to request the presence of the most powerful merfolk in the Western Atlantic—and on such short notice—is more than a little intimidating.

I dip the quill in squid ink, hold it over the page, and feel the same hesitation I experienced two days ago as I was about to sign my title away. That hesitation made me realize that I can't just walk away from my duty. I couldn't then, and I won't now.

I press the quill to the paper and start writing.

I'm only a few words in when Dosinia says, "You spelled 'requested' wrong."

"What?" I scowl.

She can't be right. She's on the other side of the table, reading upside down, and—

reqeusted

Son of a swordfish.

Meow.

Even the cat knows I'm wrong. I crumple the kelpaper into a wad and toss it behind me with the ever-growing pile of other screwups.

With a frustrated sigh—or maybe a groan, I'm not sure—I drop my head onto the table. I hear the clink of glass on wood, but I don't care. Why is this so hard? Why do I keep screwing up on something so simple but so important?

Maybe I *should* have signed my title away. Thalassinia would be better off.

"Um, Lily . . ."

My muscles tighten. Quince only uses my real name in serious situations, like when he's telling me he loves me or that I'm too good for Brody. Or—I'm guessing now—when a tipped-over pot of squid ink is seeping across the table.

"It's my hair, isn't it?" I ask, not lifting my head.

"Yeah, it's all over—" Brody grunts as something, maybe an elbow to the ribs, interrupts him.

"You look beautiful in blue," Quince says.

"Very . . . mermaidy," Shannen offers.

"I'll get a towel, dear," Aunt Rachel says.

Seconds later I feel something wrap around my hair. Holding the towel in one hand, Aunt Rachel pulls me upright with her other. Everyone at the table—Doe, Brody, Shannen, Quince—stares at me like I'm a beaten guppy. Which only makes me feel worse.

"Why don't you go take a bath?" Aunt Rachel suggests. "It will make you feel better."

And it will get the squid ink out of my hair. She doesn't say the second part out loud, but I know she's thinking it.

I stare helplessly at the mess on the table. "But I have to finish the invitations," I insist. "They need to go out tonight, or the kings and queens won't have time to make travel plans for this weekend."

"We'll get all the stamping done," Shannen offers.

Quince nods.

I shake my head. That's only part of the process.

"I'll help," Dosinia says with a long-suffering sigh, shrugging out of her magenta cardigan. "I can write the invitations."

She reaches for a stamped sheet of kelpaper and a second, unopened—and unspilled—pot of squid ink.

Prithi stretches up to rub her nose against the sweater.

I'm tempted to scowl at Doe. Since when does she volunteer, even reluctantly, to help beyond her ever-present willingness to criticize someone else's work?

But as I stare at the mess and the big smear of squid ink on Aunt Rachel's white table, I think it's probably best for me to take a time-out. If Doe actually helps, great. If not, at least I'll have a clear, calm—and clean—head when I come back down.

"Okay," I say as I stand up. "I'll be quick."

Everyone nods and goes about their work. Shannen stamping the kelpaper, Quince moving it into a row in front of Doe. Aunt Rachel mopping up the spilled squid-ink mess.

And Doe scratching a quill across the page in what looks like elegant, legible script.

At the doorway I turn back and see Brody carrying a finished invitation over to the counter, where it can dry safely.

"Thanks, guys," I say, knowing that between the bath and their support, everything will turn out fine. I hope.

2

*T*he bath is steaming hot as I step into the tub. I sink down and stretch my legs out in front of me, sighing as my body absorbs the calming effects of the water. My hair is carefully pinned up, out of the way, so the squid ink doesn't contaminate the entire tub and wind up turning my skin blue.

Closing my eyes for a second, I focus on my transfiguration as human flesh magically shifts to mermaid scales.

"Ahhhh." I smile. This is exactly what I need—a brief break from the world to relax my thoughts.

That might require a longer bath than I have time for.

Since I got back to Seaview yesterday morning, I've been thinking nonstop about the problems in Acropora. From what Tellin says, things are really bad there. His people are starving, their environment is dying, and they are leaving the kingdom in droves to seek better chances either on land or in neighboring kingdoms. Daddy confirms that Thalassinia has seen a surge in immigration; he just didn't know the reason.

Now we know why.

I shake my head and sink a little lower in the water.

How could this have been happening to the kingdom next door without us having any idea? It's sad and a little scary.

That's why I'm so eager to call the council meeting and get the other rulers involved. Everyone in the Western Atlantic should know what's happening to their kin. That Tellin's dad, King Gadus, has kept this a secret for so long has only made things worse. He let his pride hurt his people, and that's something a ruler should never do.

"But," I say to myself, "things will get better after the council meeting."

Tellin and I will make our plea as a united front, and the other kingdoms will step up to help. It's the mer-world way.

Eyes closed, I relax against the wall of the tub. I need a little more time in the water. I'll get out in a minute. Then I'll finish up the invitations and send them off by messenger gull to royal palaces across the Western Atlantic. After that, it's just a matter of figuring out what to say and waiting for the offers of help.

Meow!

My heart lurches, and I sit bolt upright in the tub. Water sloshes over the edges and onto the white tile floor.

Meow meow meow!

"Prithi," I growl at the door, where Aunt Rachel's cat is scratching to get into the bathroom. "Go stalk Doe."

She lets out a plaintive meow and then goes silent. I twist around in the tub and see the shadow of her paws under the door.

"Fine," I mutter. "Time to get back to work anyway."

Quickly transfiguring back into my legs, I lean forward and pull the plug from the drain. As the lime-scented water swirls away, I maneuver up onto my knees and turn on the faucet. I unclip my hair, lean to the side, and stick my head under the running water.

From the corner of my eye, I see dark blue running down the side of the tub. I squeeze some coconut shampoo into my hand and scrub it into my hair. Blue foam bubbles up around the drain. I keep lathering and rinsing until the foam and the water streaming from my hair have no traces of blue.

I shut off the water and quickly wrap my head in a soft, fluffy towel.

Climbing out of the tub, I grab another towel to dry off my body. I kneel down and mop up the water from the floor before tossing the soggy towel into the hamper.

Standing in front of the mirror, I pull the towel off my head and expect to see my normal blond rat's nest. Instead, I see a blond rat's nest with a giant splotch of blue on one side.

"No," I gasp.

Apparently squid ink is both water- *and* shampoo-proof. I grab the towel and scrub desperately at the discolored hair.

12

When I pull the terry cloth away and find no traces of blue, I know I'm in trouble. It's not rubbing off. My hair is well and truly dyed.

And not in a cool way. If it was just the tips or even one long streak, that would be fine. But it's a big blob. Most of the bottom half of my hair on the left side of my head. Just . . . blue.

I close my eyes and take a deep breath.

There are three options. I can cut off the blue and the rest of my hair to match, leaving me with a bob-length style. I immediately dismiss that. One disastrous experiment with short hair my sophomore year that left me looking like a fuzzy blond Q-tip taught me that lesson.

I could dye the rest of my hair to match. That would even things out, but I'm not cool enough to pull off blue hair. I'm barely cool enough to pull off normal hair.

Or I could just leave it like it is and hope it eventually fades away.

I don't like any of the options. But as I stare at the wet curls of blue and blond in the mirror, I know I don't have much choice. I will just have to live with it for a while.

Meow.

"Okay, okay," I say to the impatient cat. "I'm coming."

I get dressed and, after briefly considering—and then dismissing—the idea of fashioning the towel into a blue-hair-disguising hat, open the door. Prithi stares up at me. She blinks several times before turning and running down the hall, into Doe's room.

"That bad, huh?" I call after her.

When I walk back downstairs, I brace myself for a tsunami of comments about my blue hair. Doe's will be the worst, I'm sure. I step into the kitchen and find it empty. The table is clear, not even a trace of squid ink on the painted surface. Wish I could say the same about my hair.

Guess this explains why Prithi abandoned her Doe worship for a while.

I spin around, looking for signs of what happened, or maybe a note. I find one stuck to the refrigerator.

> *The invitations are done and the messenger gulls are on their ways. Went to get ice cream. Back soon.*
> *xoxo*
> *Rachel*

What? They finished everything? *And* they sent off the invitations via messenger gulls to the various kingdoms?

Clearly I was in the bath longer than I thought.

My heart does a little double thump. I trust my friends and family to do a good job, but . . . but I didn't even get to see a finished invitation. What if Doe worded something wrong? Or had the wrong time or location or misspelled Queen Dumontia's name? Sure, she corrected me on a couple of mistakes earlier, but she's not perfect.

I yank the note off the fridge, and a sheet of pale-blue

kelpaper that had been held up behind it falls to the floor.

It's an invitation. Stuck in the middle is a bright pink sticky note.

> *Not that you need to, but you probably want to check my work.*

Doe. I'm part annoyed by her arrogance and part relieved to see a finished invitation. I skim my eyes over the very official-sounding words.

> *Your attendance is requested at a council of mer kings and queens to be held in the royal kingdom of Thalassinia this Sunday at five o'clock Western Mer Time. Please send your reply to Mangrove at the royal palace with your intentions by Saturday evening.*
>
> Crown Princess Waterlily
> of Thalassinia

My eyes tear up as I get to the end. Everything is perfect, exactly how it should be and exactly how I was *not* making it on my own. With so much riding on this meeting, I'm beyond relieved to know the invitations are checked off the list.

Behind me, the kitchen door swings open.

"It sounds like parts are going to rattle off," Dosinia says.

"Runs just fine, dear," Aunt Rachel says. "Gets me where I need to go, and that's all I ask."

Brody tugs at his ear. "I'd ask to keep my hearing."

"I could take a look under the hood," Quince offers. "Could be just a matter of a loose gasket."

"No, really," Aunt Rachel says, "it's—"

She doesn't have the chance to finish before I rush the group and grab them all into a big hug.

"Ooof," Aunt Rachel grunts.

Quince catches everyone from the other side. "Whoa, princess."

"You guys," I say, trying to keep the emotion out of my voice, "are amazing."

I plant loud kisses on Doe, Shannen, and Aunt Rachel's cheeks. I would feel weird kissing Brody, even on the cheek, and I can't quite reach Quince, but I give him a look that says he'll be getting an even better kiss later. Doe twists out of the hug, and I reluctantly release everyone.

"It was mostly Dosinia," Shannen says, carrying the bag from the ice cream shop over to the counter, where Aunt Rachel is getting out spoons and bowls. "She told us what to do."

I turn to find Doe casually rearranging the front of the refrigerator, Prithi rubbing around her ankles as she aligns the menus and business cards and fortune-cookie fortunes that Aunt Rachel and I have accumulated over the years. I walk over to her, grab the magnet that had been holding the note and invitation in place, and put the sample invitation back where it was.

"Thank you," I say, wrapping an arm around her waist and pulling her tight, whether she wants the hug or not.

Doe shrugs, like it was no big deal.

Well, to me it is. This is my first act as crown princess, my first official royal duty, and it would have been a struggle to do it without her help.

"Come on," I say, tugging her away from the fridge, "let's have ice cream."

"Um," she says as I pull her after me, "is your hair still blue?"

I freeze on my way to the kitchen table. All eyes in the room are on me, I can feel it. This is exactly the sort of thing Doe likes to pounce on, throwing the sharpest barbs when I'm at my weakest. I brace myself for her biting comment.

"I'll fix it for you after ice cream."

The air whooshes out of my lungs. I can't have heard her right. Spinning slowly to face her, I'm sure my jaw is hanging open like an anglerfish just waiting for its unsuspecting prey to swim inside.

"Do you have a fever?" I ask. This is twice in one night she's *volunteered* to help someone. And with no real benefit for her. She must be sick.

"What?" she throws back, sauntering past me to take a seat at the table. "I probably can't get the blue out, but I'm sure I can make it look——" She looks up at me, makes a kind of swirly gesture, and winces. "Better."

As Aunt Rachel and Shannen set the bowls of ice cream

out on the table, I throw a stunned look at Quince. He gives me a kind of I-don't-know-maybe-she's-changed look in response. He's always believed in her, and maybe he's right. Maybe I need to give her the benefit of the doubt more often.

"Thanks," I say, taking the seat next to her. "I'd appreciate anything you can do."

She ignores me and slips a giant spoonful of strawberry ice cream into her mouth. She'd never admit it, but I think there's the slightest hint of a blush on her cheeks.

Quince catches my eye and winks. He saw it too.

Today my cousin is being generous, and hopefully this weekend the rulers of the mer world will be the same.

I pull my big bowl of green-tea ice cream closer and dig in. The spoon is halfway to my mouth when the reality of the situation hits me. I've called a council of kings and queens. I've made a request of the rulers of the mer kingdoms of the Western Atlantic, asking them to come to my kingdom so I can make *another* request of them.

I force the bite of ice cream into my suddenly dry mouth. If I couldn't even handle sending out invitations on my own, how on earth am I going to face a roomful of kings and queens without messing up?

I swallow the melting treat without really tasting it. I just hope that between now and Sunday, I can find the words to help me do what needs to be done. Tellin and his kingdom are counting on me, and I don't want to let them down.

3

"*I* can do this."

Staring out over the sands and surf of Seaview Beach Park, I feel like my heart is exploding in my chest. My legs shake as I step out of my flip-flops. But physical reaction aside, I actually feel pretty confident. It's the fear of public speaking—in front of a very powerful and influential public—that has me kind of freaking out.

Quince wraps a strong arm around my shoulders, steadying me. "Of course you can," he says, with so much certainty that my body relaxes a little.

I close my eyes, letting the gritty squish of wet sand massage the soles of my feet. Just a few more minutes and I'll be ready.

"You're sure you don't want me to come with you?" Doe asks.

I open my eyes to look at her. She is glued so tightly to

Brody's side, I can't see a sliver of the morning sun between them. Sure, she's volunteering—again—but I can't imagine she'd be too happy if I took her up on the offer.

"No," I say. "I'll be fine."

"Because I can, you know," she insists, pulling away from Brody a fraction of an inch. "Uncle Whelk lifted my exile."

Brody tugs her back to his side.

"I know." I give her a grateful smile. "Really, I'll be fine."

"Here," Shannen says, stepping closer. "Take these."

She holds out a stack of laminated index cards. I take them from her and quickly flip through them. They say things like "ocean warming," "request for aid," and "state of emergency." One even says "Take a deep breath."

"What are they?"

"Talking points," she says. "I always make these for my debates, to help me get back on track if I get lost. Not that I think you're going to get lost, but just in case."

I pull her into a hug.

"Thank you," I say. "Knowing I have these will help me relax, for sure."

I slip the cards into the hidden pocket in my tank top, where they will be secure for my journey home. Shannen must have spent a lot of time working on these. Her years on the debate team are definitely paying off for me.

"Besides," Brody says, trying to be helpful, "you'll have Tellin at your side. If you get stuck, he can help out."

The mention earns Brody a fuming look from Quince,

and that makes me smile. I reach for his hand and weave my fingers through his. He knows I'm not interested in Tellin, not in that way, but since I only bonded with the handsome mer prince a few days ago, it's still a new situation.

A lot has changed in those few days. Right up until the moment I was about to sign away my future as Thalassinia's queen, I thought I had my life figured out. Then, in that instant, I knew I couldn't do it. Couldn't abandon my duty, couldn't abandon my people or the people of Tellin's dying kingdom.

So, in a spur-of-the-moment decision, I kissed Tellin, bonding with him—in name only—and securing my place in the royal succession. I became crown princess, and everything changed.

Suddenly I had more duties and responsibilities than ever before. And I had something even more important: power. Not just magical power—although I got some of that too—but the power to make a difference. And my first official act as crown princess was to call a council of kings and queens of the Western Atlantic region.

At this very moment, rulers of every mer kingdom, from the edge of the Arctic to the northern coast of South America, are descending on Thalassinia for the council.

They are descending on Thalassinia . . . to listen to me.

I press a hand over my stomach.

Quince leans close. "You'll be brilliant," he whispers, and I force myself to focus on his words rather than the heat of his breath. "You are strong and smart, and most important"—he presses a quick kiss against my ear—"you care."

I nod, letting his confidence in me feed my own confidence. He's right, I do care. When I learned that Acropora—the kingdom of my childhood best friend and Thalassinia's neighbor to the south—was suffering great losses because of ocean warming, I realized that the environmental concerns affecting the planet as a whole were already causing major changes in the mer world. It's part of why I bonded with Tellin, to make sure I had the power and authority to help make a difference.

It's why I've called this council of kings and queens. To make the rest of the world aware of the problem and to secure help for Acropora. Together, the kingdoms of the mer world can make a difference.

That, more than anything else, calms my nerves. This has to be done, and if it takes making a presentation before some of the most powerful merfolk in the seven seas, then I have to suck it up and do it.

"Thanks," I whisper back to Quince. I give him a gentle squeeze to let him know he helped and then pull back. "It's probably time for me to—"

"Whoa," Shannen says, her voice an awed whisper.

She points out over the shore, to the pair of royal guards stepping up out of the surf. They are imposing—broad shouldered and big muscled. No shark in its right mind would take them on.

Doe whistles. "Being a princess comes with perks."

"Hey," Brody complains, and Doe makes a kissy face at him.

I scowl. Why did Daddy send guards?

As they emerge from the surf, the gleaming pearl buttons on their royal uniforms sparkle in the midday sun. I've had an escort of royal guards a few times, when I stayed in Thalassinia too late to go home on my own, or when I needed to leave before dawn to get back before school. But this is the first time I've had a royal escort in daylight hours.

"Double whoa," Shannen exclaims.

I follow the direction of her open-jawed stare and see another pair of guards stepping out of the sea. And another. And finally another. Eight guards in total, spines rigid and shoulders squared, stand in a line at the edge of the surf.

The only thing that ruins their intimidating military look is their legs. Below their wet-but-perfect uniform jackets, each guard sports a finkini—skin-hugging shorts made of scales the color of his tailfin.

But I'm too shocked to even giggle at their mismatched appearances. Eight guards? Since when have I ever needed more than a pair of royal guards to escort me, and then only when I'd be swimming after dark?

Echoing my thoughts, Quince asks, "Why are they here?"

"I don't know." I shake my head. "I had no idea they were coming."

The head guard steps forward. "Crown Princess

Waterlily," he says as he drops to one knee and bows his head. "I am Captain Frater of the Thalassinian Royal Guard Protection School Two. We have come to escort you home."

"Please stand," I say, urging him back to his feet quickly, before anyone notices. "I wasn't expecting an escort of guards. Is there a special reason why you're here?"

And why there are so many of you?

Frater grins and then quickly regains his stern composure. "You are crown princess now. Extra precautions must be taken, according to the royal charter."

"Oh."

I knew becoming crown princess would mean changes—beyond actually getting my crown, of course—but I hadn't expected this. Then again, I never had anything to prepare me. I have no older siblings to watch go through the process—I have no siblings, period. And it's not like I've been spending much time in other kingdoms to see how their princes and princesses make the transition to the more elevated position. I'm adrift in this situation.

"Give me a minute," I tell Frater. "You may, um, wait in the water."

"Yes, Crown Princess." He salutes and, once I return the gesture, turns and leads his school back into the surf.

"I can do this," I say, turning back to my friends.

"Nobody could do it better," Quince says with an assured nod.

Shannen steps close and lays her hands on my shoulders.

She's not usually the most nurturing type—she'd rather act as drill sergeant, keeping me on track with my studying or my homework or my (now former) crush on Brody—so I brace myself for an order or lecture of some kind.

Instead she says, "I believe in you."

I nod and then, before she can back away, I wrap my arms around her in a tight hug. Shannen is nothing if not brutally honest. If she says she believes in me, then she really does. She's not just saying it.

"Thank you," I whisper.

She pulls away. and I give her a grateful smile.

That is just the little boost in confidence I need to calm the rest of my nerves. Sure, I'm going to be making a speech in front of the mer world's most powerful rulers, but I know what I'm doing. I know that world and how it works—way better than I'll ever understand life on land. Things are going to work out just fine.

"At least you'll have good hair," Doe says, pulling away from Brody to admire her work. She reaches out to smooth a piece of my frizz. "It would be better if you'd let me weave in some green and turquoise. . . ." She tilts her head to the side and studies me. "But it definitely looks better than usual."

"Gee, thanks." I roll my eyes, even though I'm grateful for her efforts to salvage my blue hair. I self-consciously reach up to push the ends back over my shoulders.

Doe has worked a little mer magic, evening out the blue and painting it in some spots to make it look intentional. I wouldn't usually rock the blue-hair look, but the end result is actually quite pretty.

She retreats back to Brody's side, giving me and Quince some space.

"Maybe I should come," Quince says, wrapping his arms around my waist. "I can reschedule my shift."

I lift my hands to his cheeks. "No, go to work." I force an unwavering smile. "I'll be fine."

"You're sure?"

"Positive."

Lifting up on my tiptoes, I press my lips to his. I only meant to give him a quick kiss, but I linger, loving the feel of his warmth and loving him for being willing to use his *aqua respire*, even though the power to breathe water must still feel weird to him.

For one perfect moment I push the rest of the world to the side.

But I can't push them aside forever.

I pull back, loving that he follows me like he can't get enough of me, either. Time to go embrace my duty. I have a kingdom to help save.

"Want me to wish you luck?" he asks.

"Yes, please."

"Good." He presses a kiss to my forehead. "Luck." Another kiss on the tip of my nose. "Princess." He winks. "Not that you'll need it."

I sigh and rest my palm on his chest, reassured to feel the outline of the sand dollar necklace beneath his shirt. He traces my matching necklace, visible above my tank top.

"If you need me . . . ," he begins.

". . . I'll send for you."

We share one more moment before I step back, out of his embrace, and turn to face the ocean. I can't see the guards, but I know they're there. Just beneath the surface, just beyond the shore. Ready to escort me home, a crown princess facing her first official act as future queen of Thalassinia.

I force my legs not to quiver as I walk into the surf. As soon as I reach the water, as soon as the salty sea splashes over my legs, I feel instantly better. The calming effect of salt water washes away my worries. As the waves splash higher and higher, I feel calmer and calmer. More courageous and ready to face what's waiting for me in Thalassinia.

I turn to wave good-bye to my gang on the beach.

Quince, Shannen, and Brody wave back.

Doe calls out, "Don't choke!"

I throw her a thanks-a-lot scowl before turning and sinking into the sea.

The guards surround me before I've even had time to transfigure from my finkini into my tailfin. They keep their backs to me as I change, but their protection is like a solid wall around me.

"Okay," I say, once my green-and-gold tailfin is in place. "I'm ready."

Without a word to me, Captain Frater signals the other guards and they move into a diamond formation around me. He nods at me and gestures me toward the deep ocean. I kick my tailfin out behind me and head east, to Thalassinia. To home.

4

*T*ellin is waiting for me in the palace entry hall. He is studying one of the mosaic murals, the tip of his orange-to-red tailfin flicking back and forth in quick, sharp movements. Swimming through the front door feels almost exactly like that moment two weeks ago when I first saw him again after so many years. The moment that started this whole thing swimming, leading to our bond-in-name-only and to this meeting we have planned today.

I smile, realizing that I don't regret one thing.

"Tellin," I call out as I swim to him.

"Liliana," he says with a grin.

When he turns to face me, I realize he's not alone. At his side is a beautiful mermaid. She has long auburn hair that floats around her in soft curls, copper skin without a freckle in sight, and a bright teal tailfin that shimmers with flecks of pearly blue.

Tellin tugs her forward. "Lily, I'd like you to meet my mermate, Lucina."

"I am honored," she says, bowing her head. "What you have done for the sake of our people is beyond measure."

My cheeks burn with embarrassment. "It's no big deal," I say, trying to deflect the over-the-top praise. "Anyone would have done the same thing."

She lifts her head, and her eyes, the same pearly shade of blue as the highlights on her tailfin, meet mine. "No," she insists. "Your sacrifice is extraordinary, and our people will be forever grateful."

"Oh, um, well," I stammer. "You're more than welcome."

"The news of our bonding was received with great cheer," Tellin tells me. "You will forever be a heroine to the people of Acropora."

"I haven't done anything *useful* yet," I say, desperate to get off the subject of my nonimpressive heroics. "And speaking of that, why don't we go somewhere private to discuss exactly what we are planning to say in this meeting."

Tellin nods and gestures for me to lead the way. As I swim down the hall, heading for one of the antechambers that connect to the royal chamber where the meeting will take place, I take a moment to focus on the magical connection between Tellin and me.

To be honest, I've been worried. Being bonded to another merman while I'm in love with Quince . . . well, I don't know for sure what to expect. There have been plenty of bonds of convenience in the history of mer royalty, but usually the royals in question aren't dating anyone else. Definitely not dating a human.

But I had no other choice. Bonding with Tellin and becoming crown princess was the only way I could be sure to make a difference in the underwater world. I couldn't let my childhood friend and his kingdom suffer because I wanted a human boyfriend.

I'm relieved to sense nothing more than the bonds of friendship.

"Here we go," I say, swimming into the empty antechamber.

It's a small, windowless room painted a calming shade of conch-shell peach. Arranged around a low center table are four scroll-shaped chairs. I float over to one and sink down onto the stone surface.

Lucina hovers in the doorway. "I shall leave you to your planning."

I twist back to look at her.

"You don't have to go," I say, feeling awkward that she thinks she can't stay. We're not going to be discussing kingdom secrets or anything.

"No, truly," she says. "I only wished to meet you. Now I would very much like to visit the palace gardens I have heard so much about."

"I will come find you when it is done, my love," Tellin says. He presses a kiss to her cheek.

When she's gone, Tellin swims over to the chair opposite mine.

"She's lovely," I tell him. "She seems very sweet."

His smile is one of pure love and adoration. "She is an angelfish."

"I'm very happy for you." And I am. Love is a gift. I know how it feels to love and be loved in return, and I'm glad my friend can feel the same.

"Thank you," he replies. "As I am happy for you."

I give him a quick smile and then shift my focus to business. Now that we're alone in the antechamber, it hits me hard that we're about to host a council meeting. We need to talk through our plan so it goes as smoothly as possible.

"I think the meeting will be pretty straightforward," I say. "I'll start by thanking them for coming, and then . . ."

I trail off as I realize Tellin is staring at me with a very confused expression on his face.

"What?" I ask. "Did you want to start the meeting?"

"No, I . . ." He shakes his head and smiles. "You do know that your hair is blue?"

I reach up and pull my hair to one side, trying to hide the blue section behind my hands. "Yes, I know."

He nods, and I can tell he's trying to stifle a laugh.

"Can we focus on the important issue, please?" I say, tugging at my hair. I channel my embarrassment into professionalism, sitting up straighter in the chair and leveling a serious look at Tellin. "We're speaking at a council meeting in less than an hour, and I'd like to feel prepared when we swim in there."

"Yes, of course," Tellin says, his demeanor floating back to serious. "Please continue."

"As I was saying . . ." I give him a stern scowl. "After the introduction, I will turn it over to you, and you can describe the situation in Acropora. Then I will make the official request for aid."

"That sounds like an ideal plan," he says, his voice soft and sad. "I will have no trouble describing the challenges facing my kingdom."

I sigh. "I know. But just think," I say, trying to sound cheerful and optimistic, "in a short time we're going to be well on our way to getting your people the help they need."

He doesn't look quite as optimistic as I feel. "I hope you're right," he says. "I certainly hope you're right."

"I know I am," I insist. "Our kin will rise to the occasion. I'm sure of it."

"Is everyone here?" I ask, swimming back and forth in the hall outside the royal chamber.

Daddy's secretary, Mangrove, checks his clipboard. "Nearly all, Princess." He runs his finger down the list. "I believe we are missing but one."

"Let me guess." I pause my pacing long enough to look at him. "Queen Dumontia?"

"Yes, Princess."

I exchange an unsurprised look with Tellin.

Dumontia is queen of Glacialis, a mer kingdom far to the north, in the arctic waters around Canada and Greenland. She is notoriously late, and not just because she has the farthest to travel. She enjoys making an entrance.

"But the others are here?" I ask, my stomach starting to tighten. "All the kings and queens?"

Mangrove nods. "It is time."

"Oh, boy," I mutter.

Tellin reaches out and takes my hand.

"Are you ready?" he asks.

A flutter of nerves upends my stomach, but only for a second. I remind myself why I'm doing this and what I expect to happen. Everything will be fine.

"Yes," I say, squaring my shoulders. "Let's do this."

Together we turn to face the chamber door. A pair of palace guards nod and then pull open the doors as we approach.

"Your highnesses," Mangrove calls out as Tellin and I swim into the chamber, "Crown Prince Tellin of Acropora and Crown Princess Waterlily of Thalassinia."

In my most elaborate late-night imaginings, at the announcement of my entrance the entire chamber turns and stares at me, curious about the girl who dared call them to a council meeting. I imagined a mixture of anger and annoyance, and a lot of impatience.

In reality, as the echoes of the herald's announcement fade and I float into the room, no one seems to notice.

Seriously, the thirty or so merfolk seated around the council table—a wide stone slab the size of my bedroom in Aunt Rachel's house—don't stop chattering in their various groups. Eight of them are kings and queens of other mer kingdoms, while the rest are their advisers and attendants. Even Daddy is so engrossed in a discussion with jolly King Bostrych of Trigonum, Thalassinia's neighbor to the north, he doesn't realize I've arrived.

For a moment, I relish the invisibility. I scan my gaze over the chamber's occupants. Some are familiar to me; the leaders of the kingdoms nearest Thalassinia have been frequent guests at our royal events and celebrations. Others, from the more distant kingdoms, are only faintly familiar. I must have met them at state affairs once or twice, but I barely remember them. A couple are new rulers. I remember Daddy sending me notice of the death of the old king of Marbella Nova a couple years ago. One of the unfamiliar faces must be his daughter, Otaria, now the queen. And the queen of Rosmarus retired last fall, after a reign of nearly one hundred years, leaving her nephew as king. I can't remember his name.

It is a little exhilarating to be in a room with so many powerful merfolk.

"Lily," Tellin whispers, releasing my hand and nodding toward the head of the table.

I nod back. I know what he's trying to tell me, that I should stop gawking and get on with it.

I swim around the edge of the room, past the arguing king of Desfleurelle and queen of Costa Solara—the two kingdoms are neighbors and notorious rivals, so it's not surprising that they're arguing—and around the queen of Antillenes, who is in a hushed conversation with two members of her retinue.

As I pass her, my fin kick must disturb her hair, because she glances up. Her attendants look up, too, and I feel their gazes on me as I continue, taking my place at the end of the table.

Their attention must catch the notice of the other monarchs and attendants, because as I turn to face the gallery of assembled kings and queens, every single eye in the room is fixed on me.

I suck in a sharp breath.

And I thought delivering a speech in English class was terrifying.

Tellin passes behind me, taking his place at my side. One pair of eyes in the room shifts to Tellin. His father, King Gadus, does not look pleased. Tellin was not even certain if his father would be here to participate in the council. Not only because Acropora's king is ill, dying from the effects of ocean warming that are slowly but surely destroying his entire kingdom, but also because he resisted calling a council of kings and queens for so long. Until recently, he was too proud to allow even his son to ask for help. It seems he's still not entirely thrilled at the idea.

I haven't seen King Gadus for several years, but he looks decades older than the last time. His salt-and-pepper hair is thinning, his cheeks are hollow, and his skin is looser than it should be. But he's here and—if the simmering look in his brown eyes is any indication—ready for a fight.

I grip the stone table with both hands, squeezing tight to give my nerves a way out. It's not enough. My mind freezes as I confront all the faces awaiting my words—if not eagerly, then with annoyed anticipation. Everything Shannen taught me about public speaking, everything Daddy told me about making a presentation to the council, everything Quince said to help me relax, knots up in my chest, and I start to feel like I might faint.

I've never thought of myself as a coward—except where my crush on Brody was concerned, though that seems like a silly thing now—but I really don't think I can do this. My muscles tense, and I'm ready to bolt for the door, when I feel a pressure on my wrist. I look down to see Tellin's red-freckled fingers slip over mine.

I stare at our hands, and it's like a wave of calm washes up and over me. Instantly, my heart rate slows, and I can practically feel the adrenaline in my bloodstream oozing away.

I look up at him, startled.

He smiles, his eyes steady and reassuring, and I feel it. It's like his calm certainty becomes mine.

The bond. I smile back. I really needed this right now.

Taking control of my emotions, I look up and face some

of the most powerful merfolk in the seven seas. I suck in a deep breath, prepare the words in my mind, and open my mouth to speak.

"Wel—"

"What in all the oceans is this about?"

Everyone turns to look at the door, where Queen Dumontia—in all her icy-blue glory—is sweeping into the room like a wave into a tide pool. Her long, beautiful hair swirls around her, creating an aura of silvery white. The look on her face is as stark as the arctic world she rules. Stony and cold.

My stomach backflips.

"Queen Dumontia of Glacialis," Mangrove calls out belatedly, his voice quivering.

She tosses a dark look in his direction, and he quickly backs out of the chamber.

"You are right on time, Queen Dumontia," I say, trying to keep the fear out of my suddenly tight voice. "We were just about to begin."

She washes her gaze over the room, maybe to find an empty seat for herself and her bodyguards, or maybe to give everyone a nasty look. When she spots a vacant chair between King Zostero of Desfleurelle and one of Queen Cypraea's advisers, she swims over the entire table to get there.

As she settles into her seat—the bodyguards taking their places behind her, in very military-looking stances—she mutters, "I can't believe we had to answer the request of a mere child. Again." She cuts a look at King Zostero. "Probably as much a waste of time as the one *your* brat called."

The silence of the room only makes her comments resonate more.

In that moment, as scared as I am, I am also annoyed. I am not a child. I am a crown princess. It is my right—and my duty, in this instance—to call a council of kings and queens.

If she doesn't like it, then she can just deal.

I clear my throat, drawing back the attention of the room. Even Dumontia reluctantly turns her gaze on me.

I avoid that gaze as I begin.

"Welcome, kings and queens of the Western Atlantic," I say, maintaining my calm even as Tellin pulls his hand away. "Thank you for coming all the way to Thalassinia. I have called you here today to request your help. One of our sister kingdoms is in trouble"—I glance at Tellin and find him looking solemn and concerned—"but together I know we can help. Crown Prince Tellin of Acropora will tell you more about the problem."

I float back a bit to let Tellin share his part. I watch the gathered assembly as he talks about the dying ecosystem, the mass emigrations, and the bleak future of his kingdom. My emotions well up, and I expect to see matching tear-glittered eyes in the rest of the room, but I don't. Everyone is listening attentively—even Dumontia—but they look kind of unaffected.

Maybe they've learned how to mask their emotions better than I have.

When Tellin finishes his part, I float forward and prepare to make the formal request.

"As you can imagine, Acropora is in desperate need of our help." I look out over the crowd, trying to make eye contact with as many rulers as I can. "That is why we have called you here. To ask for pledges of support. What Acroporans need most right now are food and first aid, but that will only help in the short run. They also need long-term assistance in the form of broader trade routes and refuge in other kingdoms and, ultimately, in rebuilding their ecosystem."

I clasp my hands together as I finish, proud of myself for making it all the way to the end of my thoughts without stumbling once. I look out eagerly at the room.

It feels like an eternity before anyone responds. My heart beats faster, and I have to squeeze my hands tighter to keep them from shaking. I'm facing down the most powerful merfolk in my corner of the ocean—and their entourages—and they're looking at me like I've asked for a great white-themed birthday party.

When someone—Queen Dumontia, of course—finally speaks, I twirl to face her with equal parts anticipation and fear.

I shouldn't have bothered with the anticipation.

"How dare you?" she demands, and I swear I can feel her

chill all the way across the table. "To ask for generosity in times such as these? Acropora is not the only kingdom suffering the effects of environmental change."

"No, it's not."

"So are we."

"Us too."

As several kings and queens chime in, I glance around the table. "What do you mean?"

"The polar ice caps are melting," Dumontia says. "The saline concentration in our waters is fluctuating, and the plankton at the base of our food chain is dying. All levels of our ecosystem are suffering subtle but ultimately catastrophic changes."

"I—I'm sorry," I say, focusing on sounding intelligent and not standing there slack-jawed at the confession. "I didn't know."

I mean, of course I knew about melting polar ice caps. Everyone who's taken a science class in the last decade knows about melting polar ice caps. But I hadn't made the connection between that and the northern mer kingdoms.

I should have realized.

"Perhaps we can help you, too," I suggest.

"And what about Desfleurelle?" King Zostero asks. "That pipeline leak was far worse than the human news reported. Millions of gallons of oil flooded our waters, drowning surface species and coating acres of marine life with an oily film."

"You have received aid," Daddy says, and I'm grateful for him stepping in to help. "From several kingdoms, including Acropora. Can you not return the favor?"

"A reluctant handout," Zostero counters. "Your kingdom's leftovers."

"The oil reached our kingdom as well," the queen of Costa Solara chimes in. "None sent aid to us."

"That little spill is nothing to the overfishing in our kingdoms," the queen of Nephropida adds. "Every year, finding enough food to feed my people becomes more and more difficult. Not only in my kingdom's waters, but in Trigonum and Rosmarus as well."

The kings of those two kingdoms nod in agreement.

"Perhaps you should not have cut off trading with all kingdoms in the south," Daddy argues.

"You are so naive," Dumontia says to me, ignoring everyone else in the room as their voices escalate, "to think you could call this meeting and hold out your hand to help your boyfriend."

"He's not my—"

"To think one kingdom is in any greater need than another," she interrupts. "It is pure fantasy."

"I didn't mean that—"

"What do you know of the mer world anymore?"

"You've been living on land too long."

"You've grown out of touch."

"Now that is unfair," Daddy argues.

The other voices are growing so loud that I can't distinguish them.

"I must look out for my own," a voice louder than the others says. "I must take action to protect my kingdom and my people."

Then the room erupts. It's as if everyone starts talking at once, comparing stories of environmental tragedy within their kingdoms. Arguing and bickering.

I look to Tellin, helpless, but he has moved to his father's side, trying to calm the old king down as he argues with the rulers on either side of him. I float slowly back from the table.

I thought I'd been calling a meeting to request help for Acropora, a kingdom dying as ocean warming kills off their coral reefs. A simple plea for aid that I thought would be readily answered.

Instead, I find the entire Western Atlantic in environmental turmoil. Thalassinia, it seems, has been lucky so far. We are protected, carefully situated between the overfished waters to the north, the warming waters to the south, and the oil-filled waters to the west.

I've always known Thalassinia was one of the more prosperous kingdoms. I just hadn't realized we were so lucky, too.

Across the long length of the table, Tellin lifts his gaze and looks at me. He doesn't have to say a word. The bond takes care of that, of sharing his feelings with me, even at a distance. I can tell he's disappointed, and it's all my fault. I insisted we call this council of kings and queens, I insisted it was the best way to help his people. I was so sure. So confident.

So wrong.

The voices in the room get louder and the arguments swell. Each king or queen is adamant that his or her kingdom suffers the worst fate. Their shouts echo off the chamber walls until all I hear is the roar of sound vibrating through the water.

"Enough!" Dumontia's shout resonates above all the rest.

The room falls silent once more as the arguments gradually fade and the occupants turn their attention to the arctic queen.

"This," she says with a sneer, waving her hand over the table, "has been a waste of time and resources." Her eyes focus in on me. "Do not call for my attendance again."

Then, without another word, she turns and swims out the door. The wake of her fin flicks and those of her bodyguards wash through the room.

King Zostero floats up. "This has accomplished nothing," he declares before following Dumontia's path.

"No, wait," I call out, trying to salvage the purpose of this meeting. "We can still do something."

One by one, the other rulers rise from the table and storm from the room, until only Daddy, Tellin, and King Gadus are left. King Gadus tosses an angry look at his son.

"I hope you're—" A violent coughing fit cuts off his sentence. When Tellin tries to help him, Gadus knocks his hand away. The old king draws himself up straight. "I hope you're happy."

Then he follows the rest of the kings and queens.

"I—" I shake my head, overwhelmed by what just happened, by everything that I just learned is happening in my world. "I had no idea."

Then, without waiting for either Tellin or Daddy to say anything—really, what's to say?—I turn and swim away.

$\mathcal{I}$ don't realize where I'm swimming until I get there. I blindly move along hallway after hallway, around corner after corner, my mind racing with the reality of what just happened. Detail after detail replays in my thoughts, with flashes of oil spills and overfishing and melting ice caps. The scope of the problem is overwhelming. Eventually I find myself floating through the door to the map room.

I look around at the familiar room, and I'm transported to a calmer place.

This used to be one of my favorite rooms to explore in the whole palace. As I swim in, the walls on either side of the room are lined with countless drawers of maps. Ancient maps, modern maps. Maps of mer kingdoms from around the world. Human maps that have been treated with a special kind of wax to be able to survive underwater. There is even an entire stack of drawers dedicated to treasure maps.

My ancestors had a knack for talking pirates out of their secrets, and as a mergirl I dreamed of seeking out those buried boxes of gold and gems.

The most impressive element in the room, however, is the wall opposite the door. It is covered in a giant mosaic map of the world's oceans. The Atlantic is in the center of the map, with the ten kingdoms of the Western Atlantic marked by borders in the colors of each kingdom. Glacialis, far to the north, is drawn in white. Marbella Nova is a yellow-rimmed kidney bean in the south. Acropora is marked in red. Thalassinia, in the very center, is outlined in bright royal blue.

Beyond the Western Atlantic are countless other kingdoms: in the Eastern and Southern Atlantic another fifteen kingdoms; too many to memorize in the different parts of the Pacific; and a few in the Indian Ocean. And that doesn't even include those lake and river kingdoms that are landlocked on the seven continents. Well, not Antarctica—solid ice is no place for a mermaid—but the other six, anyway.

So many different kingdoms, so many different problems. And I never thought much beyond the concerns of my own shores. I can't believe I've been this . . . self-centered.

I'm ashamed that I have let myself be so disconnected from my people and my kin. Just because Thalassinia has been spared environmental catastrophe so far doesn't mean we always will be. And it doesn't mean I can bury my head in the sand and ignore what's happening in other parts of my world.

I sense Tellin entering the room before he speaks.

"It was worth a try."

I don't turn around.

"You were right," I say, floating up to the center of the map. "I was a fool to believe it would be that easy."

I trace my fingertips over the southern border of Thalassinia, where it meets the bright-red border of Acropora.

He swims up next to me. "Nothing this important is ever easy." He covers my hand with his, and together we trace our shared border. "But that doesn't mean we give up."

"I just—" I pull my hand away and float down to the floor. "I never realized how bad things were getting."

"How could you have known?"

"I could have been here; I could have taken up my duties sooner." I can feel the tears stinging at my eyes, but I can't stop them. "I could have been helping, instead of playing at being human."

Tellin sinks down next to me and wraps an arm around my shoulders. "But you *are* human," he says, giving me a squeeze. "Half, anyway. You weren't playing, you were finding yourself."

"But what if I—"

"You could not have known," a booming voice interrupts. Daddy lingers in the doorway, as if he does not wish to intrude on our moment.

"What do you mean?" I ask, swimming out of Tellin's hug. I don't want Daddy—or anyone—getting the wrong impression that my heart lies anywhere but with Quince.

"I mean," Daddy says, "that I kept the concerns of the mer world from you. I did not wish them to influence your decision."

I just stare at him, confused.

"You have your mother's compassion," he says with a smile that's just a little sad at the edges, "and her sense of justice. I wanted you to make the choices that were best for *you*, not only for your people."

"I—" This shouldn't come as a shock. Even when I was considering signing my title away to be with Quince on land, Daddy supported me without hesitation. Of course he wouldn't want the plight of my people—of my mer kin—to influence that choice. That doesn't mean I think he was right to do it, but I understand and appreciate it all the same.

"Thank you." I swim forward and wrap him in a big hug. "I wish you hadn't done that, but I get why you did."

My stomach flip-flops at the thought of how close I came to giving up my ability to help the mer world in an official capacity.

What if I hadn't decided at the last minute—the last possible moment—to bond with Tellin and save my title? What if I'd decided to stay on land and then found out later how bad things are in the ocean? I would have been devastated.

I shake my head. That doesn't matter now. I made the

right decision, that's what's important, and I'm going to make a difference.

"What are we going to do?" I ask both Daddy and Tellin.

"What can we do?" Tellin replies. There is a sadness in his eyes, a resignation that stabs me in the gut.

I look at Daddy, but he just shakes his head. He doesn't know either.

"Well, I don't know," I say. "Yet. But I'm going to figure something out." I give Tellin a confident look. "To help the mer world *and* Acropora. To get them to realize we have to work together or we will all suffer."

"In the meantime," Daddy says, "we can send some emergency supplies and aid to Acropora. I will instruct the guard to send a contingent carrying food and medical supplies with you, Tellin, when you return home."

Tellin straightens his spine and smiles. "I appreciate the offer, King Whelk."

Daddy nods and says, "I will go see to the preparations."

Then he gives me a look—I'm not sure if it's pride or concern, maybe both—before swimming out of the room. He won't say so, because he doesn't like to influence my decisions, but I can tell he's glad I made the choices I did. Not that he would have ever made me feel bad for walking away. Still, he's proud of me, I can tell. I just need to figure out how to live up to that pride.

When Daddy's gone, I turn back to the map. "The problem is so much bigger than I thought." So big it seems almost insurmountable. And this is just within our local waters. "I wonder if the other regions around the globe are suffering the way ours is."

"I have not heard anything," Tellin replies.

"That doesn't mean there aren't problems." I glance over the map, skimming over all the mer kingdoms in the far corners of the world. "They might be trying to solve them on their own, just like your father was. Just like the other kingdoms are right now."

"Here they are!"

I turn at the sound of my best friend's voice. "Peri!"

She swims into the map room with Tellin's girlfriend at her side and a school of Acroporan guards floating close behind.

"The king wishes to depart, Prince," the head guard says.

Lucina swims up to Tellin's side. "He seemed in a foul mood," she says, taking his hands in hers. "Did the council meeting go poorly?"

"You could say that," he replies.

He lowers his head until their foreheads touch, and I can't help but sigh at the gesture.

Peri leans close to my ear and whispers, "So, wanna tell me why your hair is blue?"

I wince. "No," I reply. "Actually, I don't."

She gives me a look that says I'll have to fess up eventually.

I ignore that look.

"See your father safely home," I urge Tellin. "Get the supplies Daddy is sending to your people. Hopefully that will help."

"It will," Tellin replies. "But not enough."

I give him a solemn look. "I know that. We're going to figure out what to do. We just need to regroup, to look at the problem again with what we learned today."

"I will gather my father's advisers," Tellin says. "I will tell them what happened and we will discuss our options."

"And I'll do the same," I promise. "I'll send you a gull if I figure something out."

Tellin nods. "As will I."

I watch him swim away with his girlfriend and his royal guard, and I am more determined than ever to find a solution to our problems. *All* of our problems.

Because if there's anything that the disastrous council meeting taught me—and the great mosaic in the map room reminded me—it's that all the world's oceans are really one. And a problem that faces one mer kingdom affects us all.

"So the meeting didn't go as planned, huh?" Peri asks.

I sigh out all my frustrations. "A complete conch shell from start to finish."

"Come on," she says, twining an arm around mine and guiding me from the room. "I hear Laver has some fresh kelpcakes. You can tell me all about it over some sugar and frosting."

"Sounds perfect."

I trust Peri more than just about anyone, and she's one of the smartest mergirls I know. Maybe she can help me find a solution. Even if she can't, she'll listen as I talk it through.

Laver can be very protective of his treats, so Peri and I run the play we've been practicing since we were guppies. She distracts Laver by asking him some very involved question about cooking while I sneak into the room and grab a pair of contraband goodies.

We meet up in the hallway, giggling like little mergirls as we swim away with the tasty prize.

Only this time, as we rush down the hall with key lime kelpcakes in hand, we don't make a clean getaway.

"Princess Waterlily," a mocking voice calls out as we swim toward the ramp to my bedroom. "Fleeing the scene of the disaster?"

Giggles bubble across the hall as I turn to face three of the last merpeople I wanted to see . . . ever. The terrible trio. They have matching looks of delight on their overly made-up faces.

"Don't they ever leave the palace?" I mutter under my breath. "Astria, Piper, Venus," I say, "what an unexpected surprise."

"Great white," Astria gasps with a disgusted sneer. "What happened to your hair?"

My cheeks burn, but Peri comes to my rescue.

"It's the latest thing." She smooths her fingers through

the blue strands. "Mother says every mergirl will be doing it by next month."

Being the daughter of the most popular dressmaker in the kingdom has perks when it comes to fashion. The terrible trio exchange a glance before Astria dives back in on her original attack.

So much for my reprieve.

"We heard about the council meeting," Astria says, her voice dripping with mock sympathy. "Did the foreign kings and queens really storm out in protest?"

"So dramatic," Venus says.

Piper echoes, "Dramatic."

I shake my head. "No, that's not what happened."

It's not too far off from the truth, but they didn't exactly leave in *protest*. More like in disgust.

"That's not what we heard," Astria argues. "Did Queen Dumontia really put you in your place?"

"No, she—"

"What do you know about it?" Peri blurts.

Astria's piercing gaze shifts from me to Peri. I watch my best friend, spine stiff in either terror or courage, face down one of her fiercest enemies. I'm proud of her, even though her clenched fists are shaking against her hips.

"Did you suddenly grow a backbone, parasite?" Astria sneers.

"Or maybe," Venus counters, "you're just borrowing Princess Waterlily's."

"Borrowing." Piper nods enthusiastically.

Peri drifts back an inch. I nudge myself closer to her side, letting her know she has my support.

"I will not sit silent while you disparage the name of the crown princess of Thalassinia," she says, her voice tight with emotion. "She deserves your respect."

I reach out and grab Peri's hand. She is a loyal friend, and I know how much strength it's taking for her to stand up to her childhood nemesis.

"Respect is earned," Astria throws back. "And not by calling a council of kings and queens in which all the kings and queens flee in anger."

"Anger," Piper parrots.

"Shut up, Piper," Astria snaps.

Piper's eyes widen as she blinks in shock. This can't be the first time Astria has turned on her own.

"You don't know anything about it," Peri insists.

Astria floats closer, until she's just inches away from us. "I know that if *our princess* had spent more time with the royal tutor and less time falling in love on land, she might have done a better job with her first official duty."

I'm not sure who is more stunned: me, Peri, or Piper, who is still reeling from Astria's shutdown. For several long seconds we're all silent.

I don't know what the others are thinking—except Piper, who probably isn't thinking much of anything—but I'm processing a mix of shame and anger and absolute frustration.

Partly because I think Astria is right, partly because everything that happened in the last few hours has built up to the point where I just have to let it out.

"Enough!" I shout.

Everyone floats away from me. At first I think it's because of my outburst, but then I realize the water around me is swirling. I don't notice at first, the motion is so subtle, but then I feel the whirlpool forming.

I take a moment to absorb the sensation. I knew that ascending to my new title would come with new powers, beyond the ordinary mer powers of transfiguration and controlling water temperature. I just didn't know what controlling the movement of water would feel like. It feels . . . exciting.

It also feels dangerous.

This is how ships disappear on smooth seas—mer powers gone out of control. I clench my jaw and force some calm into my mind. Peri's hand squeezes mine, and I look at her. Her gray-green eyes are wide—not with shock, but with awe. She knows exactly what's happening.

The connection with her brings me back into control. I drag in a deep breath and let it out before I continue, making sure I keep my emotions in check while giving the terrible trio a big piece of my mind.

"Don't you have something more worthwhile to do," I ask Astria, "than grub around the palace looking for gossip?"

She opens her mouth to answer, but I don't let her. This

is my moment, and I'm going to say what I've wanted to say for years.

"You think *I'm* out of touch with the world down here?" I curl my tailfin. "You have no clue. The oceans are changing, mer kingdoms are suffering, and our kin are dying."

Astria's facade falters.

"Are you doing anything to help? Or are you wasting your energy picking on mergirls you think won't fight back?" I continue, pushing away from Peri and edging Astria back toward her companions with an extra surge of water—I can definitely get used to this new power. "Well, that ends now. If you want to be welcome in this palace, you will treat the merfolk within with respect. Or I will make sure you never enter again."

"You can't—"

"Can't I?" I reply, before Astria can finish her sentence.

"You won't," Venus says weakly.

"Won't," Piper whispers. Then she turns to her friends. "My dad would kill me if I got expelled from the palace."

Astria tilts her head slightly to the side, pursing her lips as she studies me. Like she's weighing the options of her response.

To my surprise, her better judgment wins out.

"Of course, Princess," she says, bowing her head in slightly less mocking respect than usual.

Her mirror images do the same, muttering quietly, "Yes, Princess."

I bite back a smile.

"Now, if you'll excuse us," I say, tugging Peri's hand and swimming around the three mergirls I used to be afraid of, "we have a very important appointment."

We maintain our composure until we get halfway up the ramp to my bedroom. Then we explode into giggles.

"Oh my gosh," I burst. "That was kind of awesome."

"Kind of?" Peri echoes. "Try very!"

We're laughing as we swim into my room. Floating to my bed, we curl up next to each other in the giant shell. I begin peeling the paper off my kelpcake.

"Thank you," Peri says, delicately pulling the paper from her cake and setting it on my bedside table.

"For what?" I ask.

"For standing up for me," she says quietly.

"Me?" I say, my kelpcake halfway to my mouth. "You stood up for me. Twice. That was amazing."

Peri shrugs. "I guess we stood up for each other."

"Always," I say before taking a giant bite out of my kelpcake.

"Now," Peri says, inspecting her treat to find the ideal first bite, "what happened at the council meeting? Was it as bad as Astria said?"

"Oh, Peri," I say around my mouthful of kelpcake, so it sounds more like "Oh, berry." I swallow my ambitious bite. "It was awful."

"Tell me all about it." She leans her head on my shoulder.

"And don't leave out the part about why your hair is blue."

I smile as I rest my head on top of hers and start spilling the details. Too bad changing the past isn't one of my new powers.

$\mathcal{T}$he royal guard wants to escort me all the way back to my house, but I convince them to leave me at the beach. Not only would a group of military-jacket-and-finkini-wearing soldier dudes make more of an impression than I'd like, I also want the alone time. The plan was to call Quince when I got back to the beach. He would come pick me up and drive me the two miles back home.

But as I watch the guards dive back into the ocean, all I want to do is take that long walk in the moonlight.

I feel so disappointed, like I'm such a failure. A selfish failure. Am I really so naive to think that just calling mer kings and queens into a meeting will solve a problem as big as the changing environment? Or that they aren't facing huge problems of their own?

I can hardly blame them for storming out the way they

did. If I were in their positions, I might have done the same thing.

That doesn't mean I'm going to let it end like that. The mer world needs help, and I'm going to find a way to make things better. To make the rulers see that working together is our only hope. This is my duty and my mission.

Scuffing my flip-flops along the sidewalk, I stare up at the starry night above. The sky looked just as clear and peaceful and welcoming the first night I spent in Seaview. Almost four years ago, I left the only world I'd ever known to come live on land, to live among humans, and to find out more about my mom's world.

Now I'm practically a woman. I am a crown princess and a girlfriend and a half-human mermaid who sees a big problem in the world and is determined to fix it. I just need to figure out how to do that.

The distant roar of a motorcycle brings me out of my fog, and I turn to see a single headlight shining from the beach end of the street. I stop, smiling, as Quince rolls up on Princess and pulls over in front of me.

The boy sure does know how to rock a leather jacket and a pair of biker boots. He pulls off his helmet and hangs it on a handlebar.

"I thought we had a plan, princess," he says without accusation.

"I know." I shake my head. "I needed some time to think."

Quince cuts the engine and climbs off the motorcycle. "Bad?"

"I don't know what I was thinking," I say. "I thought it would be so easy."

He stuffs his hands into his back pockets. "Want to talk about it?"

"No," I say, stepping forward and slipping my arms around his waist. As I lay my head against his chest, I sigh. "I want to go back to yesterday and tell myself not to be so stupid."

"Lily," Quince says, his disapproval rumbling in his chest, "you're not stupid."

"Fine, naive," I say, trying to pull away, but Quince tugs me back. "I'm an eighteen-year-old princess." I roll my eyes at myself. "What do I know about interkingdom politics? Or widespread environmental disasters? Or even how to talk to a roomful of people without freaking out like a fraidy fish?"

Quince is silent for so long, I finally pull back and look at him, half afraid I'm going to see pity and disappointment on his face. That's how I feel, anyway. But instead I see strength and confidence.

"If there are two things I know about you, Lily Sanderson," he says, his mouth kicking up into that smirky half smile, "it's that you are persistent and you have a good heart."

I sigh. "How do either of those things help me?"

"They won't solve your problem," he says. "But they will make sure you keep trying until you do."

"Sometimes you don't make any sense," I tell him.

He laughs, and his good mood relaxes me. "Maybe not," he says. "But I'm always right."

"Always?" I ask with a raised brow.

He nods, leaning in close to whisper, "Always," against my lips.

He might not make sense, but he believes in me.

"You want a ride?" he asks. "Or should I roll along beside you like a creepy stalker?"

I scrunch up my face, like I'm trying to decide. "Well, you do have a history of peeping in my bathroom window. . . ."

"I never saw a thing." He lets his gaze drift over me, and I feel my skin tingle all over. His voice is low as he says, "Promise."

I turn and saunter toward the motorcycle. I call out over my shoulder, "Did you ever stop to think that maybe *I* was the one doing the watching?"

Quince's booted footsteps thud on the concrete as I open the storage compartment on his bike and pull out my pink helmet. I'm not startled when his arms wrap around me from behind.

"I always knew you had a bad-girl streak," he murmurs against my ear.

I smile and lean back into him. "Only for you."

"Wouldn't want it any other way." He presses a warm kiss onto the side of my neck. "Come on," he says, stepping back and grabbing his helmet off the handle. "Let's go home."

I nod and climb onto Princess behind him. It's late, it's been a stressful day, and I still have a lot of thinking to do. Somehow I have to figure out how to get a diverse group of kings and queens to stop bickering long enough to realize that helping one another is the only solution to the environmental problems facing our world. That's a tall order, even for a princess with a bad-girl streak.

By morning, I have the beginnings of an idea. Not an idea of what to do, exactly, but an idea of who I can talk to who might. Seaview High's earth science teacher has been trying to help me plan my future, and she just happens to have a degree in marine biology. Maybe she can help me shape my beginnings of a plan, too.

Besides, after ditching two important interviews she set up for me recently, I owe her a big apology.

I knock on her open classroom door. "Um, Miss Molina?"

"Yes?" She looks up, sees me, and frowns a little. "Lily."

I can tell she's disappointed. And maybe a little upset. That's totally understandable. When I thought I wanted to give up my crown and stay on land, I decided marine biology would be an ideal—and obvious—career path. Miss Molina studied marine biology in college and still has connections in the department at Seaview Community College. She went out of her way to set up—and then reschedule—an interview with her friend there.

She didn't have to help me, but she did. Then I had to

bail on both interviews for various mer-world emergency situations.

I can't exactly explain how two weeks ago I'd planned to stay on land and go to college and have a career, and now I'm taking up my duties as a mermaid princess so I won't be needing her connections at the community college after all. I have no choice but to let her be disappointed in me. I just hope she can see past that and still help me.

"I know that you're mad that I missed the second interview," I blurt before she can say anything. "You have every right to be. I can't give you a good excuse, except that an urgent family situation came up at the last minute."

She closes her eyes and sighs. That's the same lame—and yet not untrue—excuse I gave the first time. She probably thinks I'm totally full of it, and if I were her I'd think so too.

No way is she going to want to help me after I made her look bad to her friend at the college.

I'm about to turn around and abort my plan, to find some other way to get advice, when she opens her eyes and half smiles. She rubs her lips together for a second and then nods.

"I know you're not a flake, Lily," she says. "If you had to miss the interview, I'm sure you had a good reason."

If she only knew.

"I'm really sorry," I repeat. "I hope your friend isn't mad at you because of me. I can talk to her and tell her that it was all my—"

"It's fine, Lily," she says, waving me into the room. "Really."

I give her a grateful smile for forgiving me as I drop into the chair next to her desk.

"Actually, I have something else I wanted to talk to you about," I say. "I need some advice."

Now I have to figure out how to present the problem.

Last night as I stared out my bedroom window for hours, counting stars, I let my mind drift, thinking about everything that's happened in the last few weeks. I got over my crush on Brody and started my relationship with Quince. I nearly gave up my crown and then bonded with Tellin so I could keep it. I thought I wanted nothing more than to return to Thalassinia with Brody at my side, then decided to stay on land with Quince, and finally realized I couldn't abandon my royal duties like that. All that thinking left me a little uncertain about where I'm supposed to be, exactly— land, water, both?—but I'm starting to think it can't be one or the other with me.

Anyway, as I thought about my now-discarded plans to become a marine ecologist, to get a degree in marine biology so I could help save the oceans from my place on land, I thought about how Miss Molina had been so willing and eager to help me with my college plans. . . . Maybe she would be able to help me with my current problem, too.

As soon as I'd decided to ask her for help, my mind turned off, and I fell asleep.

Now, faced with actually doing the asking, I wish I'd stayed awake long enough to figure out this part of the plan.

Probably the easiest way is to be as honest as I can.

"A lot of things have changed in my life in the last couple weeks," I begin. "And I don't think that going to college is going to be part of my plan."

"Are you certain?" she asks. "Getting a higher education is the doorway to far greater career opportunities."

I rub my itchy palms against the edge of my seat. I knew this was going to be a tricky part of the conversation. The teachers at Seaview High seem to be on a mission to get every single student to college. In most cases, I think this is a great goal. But not every kid needs college. Some of them just need to work. Like Quince. They gave up on him a while ago—he already has a job in construction lined up, and there's not much a college degree is going to do for him.

A college degree isn't going to help me rule Thalassinia, either. Human higher education doesn't offer classes in mer politics, and that's what I need to learn to become a better future ruler. Not that I can share that bit about my plans with Miss Molina.

"I'm sure," I say, hoping she'll leave it at that. "But the thing is, I still want to make a difference in the oceans. I still want to help the environmental efforts. I just don't know how to make that happen."

She purses her lips again and glances at the ceiling, thinking. I sit quietly and wait.

"It is true that the scientific community represents only one facet of the efforts to preserve the world's oceans." She pulls open her bottom desk drawer and starts flipping through the files. "There are a number of nonprofit organizations that are always eager for volunteers."

"That's great," I say, "but . . . well, I was kind of thinking about starting my own organization."

She pauses her search and looks up, surprised.

"Oh, nothing big or anything, just me and my friends." And by "friends," I mean the most powerful merfolk in our part of the ocean, who aren't exactly feeling friendly toward me right now.

I sit on my hands so they don't start fidgeting with the hem of my skirt.

"I don't understand," Miss Molina says. "What are you asking from me?"

"Advice," I say, leaning forward. "Some of my friends think the problems are too big for us to make a difference. They see ocean warming and oil spills and overfishing and just want to give up."

"Ah, I see."

"How do I convince them that we can change things for the better?" I give her a shaky smile. "How do I get them working together toward a common goal?"

"You're serious about this?" she asks, like she's gauging my commitment. Like she's trying to find out if I'm just going to bail on this like I did on the interviews.

"Absolutely," I say. "As if my entire world depended on it."

She studies me for a moment, lips pursed and thinking. Maybe she wonders why I'm so adamant about this, and I wish I could explain it. To her I must just look like some random high schooler who happens to be focused on saving the oceans at the moment and will probably change her mind next week. And the week after that. And every week for the next three years. She doesn't realize that the ocean isn't a passing fad for me—it's my home. And I'm going to do whatever I can to protect the mer world and my people.

My determination must read on my face, because she finally nods.

"If you want to get everyone working toward the same end," she says, "the first thing you need to do is define the scope of your mission."

"How do I do that?" I ask.

"There are two parts to any mission statement," she explains. "First, you need to define what problems you want to tackle. Are you interested in keeping the oceans clean? Or counteracting the effects of climate change? Or reducing the impact of human activities on the marine ecosystem?"

"Yes." I nod. "All of the above."

"Then you need to document each problem as thoroughly as possible." She braces her forearms on her desk. "Do some research so you know exactly what you're facing."

"Like a survey or something?" I ask.

"Exactly."

"Okay," I say. "And then second part?"

"Determine how you are going to try to solve each problem," she explains. "What actions are you going to take, and how are you going to measure and define your success?"

"Okay, that makes sense." I realize I'm fidgeting with the hem of my skirt and stuff my fingers back under my thighs. "What if my first goal is just to get other people—my friends—involved and committed to the problem?"

"That is always a difficult part of the process."

She reaches back into her file drawer and pulls out a thick green folder. Flipping to the very back, she pulls out a pale-blue sheet of paper. As she holds it out for me to see, she says, "Perhaps you can begin with something as simple as a petition."

I take the paper from her and study it. At the top it says ENVIRONMENTAL CLUB, and then it explains what the petition is for, to document interest in the formation of the club at Seaview High. Below that is a list of names, signatures, and student numbers, about twenty-five in all. And at the very bottom is a place for the club sponsor, Miss Molina, and the school principal to sign.

"This is how you started the environmental club?" I ask.

She nods. "What you are trying to accomplish is quite a bit more complicated, but getting pledges of support in writing could be a starting point."

"So—do research to define the scope of the problems," I say, handing the petition back to her. "Then get my friends to commit in writing?"

"It's as good a place to start as any."

"Thank you," I say. "That helps a lot."

She smiles. "I'm always here if you need me."

As I push to my feet, I say, "I'm sure I will."

I feel relieved as I head out into the hall, now filling up with before-school traffic. I know what my first two steps have to be. They won't be easy, not after the disaster that was my council of kings and queens, but if I can get an idea of exactly what problems we're facing and then convince everyone to agree that we need to work together to solve them—if I can make each of them see that focusing on his or her kingdom's problems alone isn't going to solve things in the long run—well, then, that's a start.

The crisis facing the mer world isn't separated by imaginary borders on the seafloor. It affects us all. And it's going to take all of us working together to make a change.

7

"*A*re you sure you know what you're doing?" Shannen's voice is a little higher than usual as she buckles her seat belt.

"Absolutely," I lie. "I've been practicing."

She gives me a skeptical look and tugs her belt tight. I flash her a sunny smile and turn the key in the ignition. In truth, I've only had the car—*my car*—a few days and haven't had much time for driving lessons. But I've been watching Aunt Rachel for years. How hard can it be?

"I have to be better at driving a car than a motorcycle," I say as I put the car into reverse.

Despite Quince's diligent effort over the past few weeks, the best I've managed on Princess is getting her started and sputtering forward until she dies, because I don't know how to operate the clutch properly.

Shannen's eyes widen.

Okay, maybe not the best argument.

"I made it *to* school just fine this morning."

Shannen wraps her arms around her backpack, clutching it to her chest. Clearly my reassurance hasn't made her feel any better about my driving ability. I will just have to show her my skill.

Watching carefully over my shoulder, I back out of the spot in the remote corner of the school parking lot—as far from other cars as possible. When I'm clear of the lamppost, I shift into first.

"See," I say, grinning, "I've totally—"

As I release the brake, the car lurches forward, jerks back, and dies.

"Damselfish." Guess I released the clutch instead of the brake. If I could just get this clutch thing figured out, I'd be an ace driver. I don't have a problem operating the one on a wakemaker back home, so I should be able to do it on land.

I quickly correct my mistake, and soon I'm driving us out of the parking lot and down the street toward home.

"I've got it now," I insist.

Shannen whimpers as I slam to a halt at the next stop sign. It's fine. That's what seat belts are for.

"Thanks for offering to help," I say, trying to get her mind off my driving. "I've never done anything like this before and—"

"Lily!"

A woman on a bicycle darts out in front of me, and I have

73

to swerve to keep from splatting her onto the sidewalk. My tires squeal to a stop. As my heart freaks out in my chest, I turn to glare at the dangerous cyclist.

Completely unaffected by the near accident, the bicycle rider—a woman with short brown hair—turns and looks at me. And smiles.

"Oh no," I whisper.

"What?" Shannen asks, eyes clenched shut. "Did you kill her?"

I frown at her. "No," I grumble. "I didn't even touch her."

"Then what?"

I suck in a deep breath as the woman throws me a jaunty wave before continuing down the street toward my house.

"I didn't hit her," I say, a knot tightening in my stomach. "I know her."

The bicycle is leaning against my front porch when I lurch to a stop against—okay, *on top of*—the curb. I cut the engine, grab my bag from the backseat, and stomp up the driveway to the kitchen door. I think Shannen is frozen solid after my race home. I'm not worried about her right now. She'll come inside when she's ready.

"Calliope," I call out as I fling open the door. "Where are you? Calliope!"

Dosinia appears in the doorway between the kitchen and the living room. "Do you have to shout?"

I glare at her. "What are you doing home?" I demand.

"Aren't you usually cozying up to Brody at the Five and Bean after school?"

"We got our lattes to go." She crosses to the fridge and takes out the pitcher of lemonade. "Aren't you usually failing miserably at riding a motorcycle after school?"

I glare at her back as she pours lemonade into a clean glass. She and I don't hate each other as much as we used to—and not just because she's bonded to my former crush and actually seems happy for once—but she still knows how to push my buttons.

Right now I don't have time to trade jellyfish barbs with her.

"Where is she?" I demand.

Doe turns to face me and jerks her caramel-blond head in the direction of the living room. "Is she always so . . . peppy?"

I lift my shoulders in a heavy sigh. "Yes," I say. "Always."

"Hi, Shannen," Doe says, looking over my shoulder. "Got a ride home with Lily, did you?"

I turn and see Shannen, wide-eyed, nodding her head.

"I wasn't *that* bad," I insist. Shannen's eyes get even wider. Fine, I was *that* bad. But I had my reasons. "You settle in at the table," I suggest, hoping that giving her something to focus on will make her forget our near-death experience with the garbage truck. I did stop in time. "I have to go find out why she's here; then we can get started."

Shannen doesn't respond, but she drops her backpack on

the table and sits in the nearest chair. I'm not sure which is more disconcerting: her blank-eyed stare or the fact that she doesn't immediately open her backpack and start in on homework.

"Here, take this to our guest," Doe offers, pushing the lemonade into my hand. "I'll fix another glass for Shannen."

I'm too distracted to worry about Shannen's shock or wonder at Doe's uncharacteristic generosity. I nod in thanks and head into the living room.

Calliope Ebbsworth is sitting on Aunt Rachel's floral sofa next to Brody, reading a scroll of kelpaper that reaches all the way to the floor, with Prithi purring contentedly in her lap. My first real interaction with Calliope—the foremost mer couples counselor in Thalassinia—was when Quince and I were accidentally bonded while I thought I was still in love with Brody. Daddy made us go through the motions with Calliope to make sure I really, really, *really* wanted to break the bond with Quince.

At the time, I did. But her methods definitely helped me see the truth about Quince and helped me realize my own feelings for him, feelings I'd never even let myself imagine.

Why she is here now, when I'm perfectly happy with Quince—bond or no—is confusing. Maybe she's here to counsel Dosinia and Brody. Or maybe she wants me to do some exercises to make sure my bond-in-name-only with Tellin doesn't muddy my emotional waters with Quince.

"Hello, Calliope," I say, walking into the living room.

"Princess Waterlily," she replies with a grin. She releases the top of the kelpaper scroll, and it rolls down to join the rest of itself on the floor. Prithi startles and makes a dash for the stairs. "Just the mergirl I wanted to see."

There goes the hope she's here for Doe and Brody.

"I'm also the mergirl who almost ran you over with her car." I hand her the lemonade before taking a seat in the recliner next to the sofa. "You have to be careful on your bicycle."

"Oh, you know." She waves her hand at me like it's no big deal. "A fish on a bicycle."

She laughs at her own joke, and I wait while she takes a long drink.

"Shannen might never recover," Doe says. She crosses to the sofa and squeezes in between Brody and Calliope. "You've scarred her for life."

Brody chuckles as he hands Doe one of the coffee cups he's holding.

I glare at her.

She takes a sip of her latte and slips her free hand into Brody's. When he makes a swoony smile at her, I turn my attention back to Calliope.

"What's going on, Calliope?" I ask, hoping this will be quick and easy so I can get to work with Shannen on developing the survey I'm going to take to the mer kingdoms. "Why are you here?"

"Can't a mermaid come visit her princess without a

reason? Your hair is looking particularly lovely today. Have you done something to it? Is it shorter?"

"Calliope . . ."

Her chipper expression turns serious.

"Well . . ." She glances down at the kelpaper scroll at her feet. "It seems there is a bit of a legal knot surrounding your bond to Prince Tellin."

The muscles in my shoulders tighten. "What kind of knot?" I demand. "Bonds in name only happen all the time in the mer world. I know I'm not the first."

"Certainly not," she says with a sympathetic smile, "but you are the first in recent memory to do so openly, and with a human mate already at your side. It is a unique situation."

"Okay," I say, really not liking the sound of this. "What does that mean?"

She sets her glass on the table and grabs the scroll off the floor. "At your father's request, his advisers and I have been reviewing the ancient laws of royal bonding. It seems our ancient mer founders foresaw such a possibility and set up a kind of—" She clears her throat. "Requirement."

"What kind of requirement?" Her avoidance is making me all kinds of nervous. "More bond counseling? Another couples challenge?"

Thinking back to the time Quince and I spent on Isla Amorata, I don't count that as much of a punishment. We could use some romantic alone time on a tropical island.

"No, dear. Unfortunately it requires a great deal more than that."

Is that sympathy I hear in her voice? My hands start shaking.

"What?" I ask, my voice softer. "Just tell me, Calliope."

"It seems the ancient law requires your human to . . ." She shakes her head. "He must pass the Trial of Truth."

Doe gasps.

"What?" Brody asks.

I suck in a tight breath. The Trial of Truth? I've heard rumors of this all my life, but I never believed it was really real. I never believed anyone would actually have to face that.

Especially not anyone I love.

The Trial of Truth is supposed to be the ultimate test of a human's love for a merperson. In order to prove his worth, the human must pass three ridiculously hard tests, tasks that are nearly impossible if the human does not have the strength of true love driving him.

The thought of Quince going through that makes me nauseous.

The thought of him failing is even worse.

"No," I say, shaking my head. "There must be a way around it. Can't Daddy do something? Make some royal decree or pass a new law?"

"You know that isn't possible." Calliope inches forward

on the couch, closer to me, and rests her hand on my knee. "The ancient law is immutable."

"What's the Trial of Truth?" Brody asks.

Doe sets her coffee on the table and whispers, "I'll explain later."

My mind races. I try to remember everything I know about ancient law and mer bonding. But the truth is I'm not an expert in these things. Maybe if I'd stayed in Thalassinia instead of living on land for nearly four years, if I'd gone through all the royal training I *should* have gone through before my eighteenth birthday, then I would have been able to avoid this.

Of course, then I never would have met Quince, and he wouldn't be facing this anyway.

I force my shoulders to relax, and I take a calming breath. There's nothing I can do about the past now. I don't have any regrets—although a small part of me really wishes I'd never severed the bond with Quince. Things would be so much easier for both of us right now if we were legally bonded.

But no, I know why I made my choice. I refuse to tie Quince to me, to my location and my body form, for the rest of his life. He has his mom to look out for and a future on land. He needs to be free to come and go from the sea, while I will be spending more and more time in Thalassinia, fulfilling my royal duties.

I hope Quince will come with me as much as he can, but it needs to be his choice.

"Okay, Calliope," I say, steeling myself. "We can do this."

"Of course you can," she insists.

"Quincy is strong," Doe offers. "If anyone can pass the Trial of Truth, he can."

I smile gratefully. My baby cousin might be a brat and a pain in the tailfin most of the time, but she knows how to step up when I need her.

"Will someone please tell me what's going on?" Brody demands. "Why are you three acting like someone died?"

Doe leans close and whispers in his ear. As she explains the situation to him, his eyes widen and he gives me a pitying look.

"It'll be fine," I say, trying to stay positive.

Doe is right. Quince is strong, and so is his love. He will pass these tests, I know he will. That doesn't mean they won't be hard and I won't worry about them, but it *will* be fine.

"Hey, Lily?"

I turn at the sound of Shannen's voice. The terror is gone from her eyes, and she looks like her normal, down-to-business self again.

"Do you want to work on this tomorrow?" She glances at Calliope and back at me. "If you have stuff to do . . ."

"No," I say, eager to get to work on the other big problem in my life. I can't do anything about the trial right now, but I can make progress on the survey. I look back at Calliope. "We're done here, right?"

81

"Yes." Calliope gathers her scrolls into her bag. "Now it is just a matter of waiting for the call to the first test."

I join Shannen at the kitchen table, where she has pens and notepaper laid out and her laptop open, ready to work. When I told Shannen about Miss Molina's advice, she volunteered to help me create the survey to make documenting the environmental problems easier. She's a whiz at anything that involves research and organization, so I really appreciate her help. If only she were a whiz at the mer kingdoms of the Western Atlantic, too.

Calliope walks through on her way to the door. "I really am sorry I had to be the bearer of this news, Princess," she says. "You and Quince deserve some peace and happiness."

"I know."

"And I really do love your hair." She smiles. "The blue is a lovely shade."

I smile back. "Thanks."

"Is there anything I can do to help?"

"No, I—" I shake my head, my gaze drifting to the work before me on the table. Speaking of experts in all things mer world . . . "Actually," I say, looking up at her expectantly, "I could use your advice on something else. Can you stay for a while?"

She immediately drops her bag to the floor and slips into the chair next to me. "Of course. What can I do?"

8

"*Y*ou're nuts," Dosinia snaps. "You need to get the support of Glacialis first. Queen Dumontia is the most respected ruler in the Western Atlantic."

I roll my eyes. "Glacialis is too far away," I say, for what feels like the tenth time. "It will take most of a day to even get there. If I start with her this weekend, then that will be the only thing I accomplish."

"Exactly," Calliope says, coming to my defense. "If Lily begins closer to home, in Trigonum and Desfleurelle and Antillenes, she can speak with three kingdoms right from the start."

"But without Glacialis, she might not *get* their support," Dosinia returns.

Prithi can't decide which mermaid to love on. She moves in a triangle, weaving around my ankles, then Doe's and Calliope's, and back to mine. She must be in kitty-cat heaven.

Shannen and Brody exchange a look across the kitchen table as the three of us mergirls erupt in an animated debate. We're so fixed on talking over each other, jabbing our fingers at the map of the Western Atlantic laid out across the table, that I don't hear the door open.

"I'm just trying to save her from looking stupid later," Doe argues.

"And I'm trying to help her make the most of her time," Calliope returns.

"I never know what I'm going to find when I walk through this door."

I look up at the sound of Quince's voice. "Hi—"

"She might as well tear up the surveys right now," Doe continues, "if she's going to start with those lesser kingdoms."

I throw a warning glare at Dosinia. "They are not *lesser*," I grind out. "They are smaller and not as wealthy as some of the others."

Dosinia crosses her arms over her chest and purses her lips. "I think the word you're looking for," she says defiantly, "is *lesser*."

I growl, debating whether crawling over the table to strangle her would count as mermicide. Surely a jury of anyone who's ever met my bratty cousin would understand.

I roll my eyes—again—and am about to start in on her—*again*—when Quince notices our visitor.

"Calliope?" He throws me a questioning look. "What

brings you to our fair shores?"

Everyone around the table suddenly clams up. Quince walks behind me and places his hands on my shoulders. He starts rubbing, like he can sense how tense the situation is making me.

"What?" he asks. "Bad news?"

I try to force myself to relax, to urge him to relax, too. The tension swirling around the room doesn't help. I catch Doe's eye and lift my eyebrows in a suggestive gesture. Amazingly, she gets—and *takes*—the hint.

"Brody, didn't you need some help with your econ homework?" Doe asks.

She reaches down and scoops Prithi into her arms—I knew she was developing a soft spot for the cat.

Brody shoves back from the table. "Oh, right. Yeah, let's go work on that."

In a flash, they're both gone.

"I need to get going," Shannen says, stuffing her laptop into her backpack. "I have a ton of calculus homework to do. You'd think, with there only being a couple weeks left in school, Mr. Kingsley would lay off, but I think it's his mission to keep us drowning in busywork right up until graduation."

She heaves her backpack onto her shoulder, gives me a sympathetic look, then says good-bye and slips out the kitchen door.

With the table empty except for me and Calliope, Quince

drops casually into the seat Shannen vacated, resting his arm on the back of my chair.

"Okay," he says, sounding calm, "just tell me. What's going on?"

Calliope starts to explain. "Well, you see, according to ancient mer law, when a mer prince or princess falls in love—"

I touch her on the arm, and she stops. This is my guy. I'm the one who got him into this, and I'm going to be the one to tell him about it. It's my responsibility.

"It's called the Trial of Truth," I say. "It's a test of . . . worthiness, I guess, that the ancient founders of mer society dreamed up for situations like ours."

"When a mermaid princess and a human fall in love?"

I twist in my chair and lay my arm over his, smoothing my fingertips across the soft leather. I shake my head as I explain. "When they are already in love when the mermaid princess bonds to another merman."

His Caribbean-blue eyes study me, unblinking. I force myself to keep the fear hidden. The trial is going to be hard enough for Quince. I don't want my worries to stress him out even more.

"What do I have to do?" he asks.

For this answer, I turn to Calliope. She knows more about what exactly everything will entail.

"It is a series of three tests, designed according to specifications written by the ancient rulers of the original five mer kingdoms." Calliope pulls out the kelpaper scroll and searches for the part that explains the process. She reads, "'The human mate must complete the three tests within one lunar cycle of bond formation to prove worthy of the mer-folk's love.'"

"One lunar cycle," he repeats. "That's—"

"Four weeks," I say. "From the time of the bond. From my birthday."

He nods. "Okay, so three weeks from now. What are the tests?"

"That I can't tell you," Calliope says. "They will be delivered to you when the time is appropriate."

"Instructions will be sent by messenger gull," I explain. "Directly from the royal chamber at the palace."

Quince lets out a humorless laugh. "Do I get any hints?" he asks, and though he's trying to play it light, I can tell he's worried. "Don't tell me I have to go into this totally blind."

"No, of course not," I say, giving Calliope a meaningful look.

"No, no," she says. "I can tell you that of the three tests, one will challenge you physically, one will challenge you mentally . . ."

"And the third?" Quince asks.

"The third will challenge you emotionally."

"What does that mean?" I ask.

"It will test the strength of your love." Calliope gives us

a brilliant smile. "And after having worked with you both before, I am sure that will be the easiest of the three."

Quince squeezes my hand. "No problems there."

He's taking this really well, and maybe that's because he doesn't yet understand how difficult these tests will be. There's no point in worrying him now. He'll find out eventually, when the instructions come. And either he'll handle them . . . or he won't. There's nothing we can do about it now.

I refuse to even consider the possibility of failure.

Calliope gets up from her chair. "I should return to the kingdom. I'll leave you two to discuss things." She lifts her tote bag onto her shoulder and reaches in to dig something out. "I am quite sure you will meet the Trial of Truth without difficulty," she says, and I hope Quince doesn't notice the waver in her voice, "but should you need anything—anything at all—you can send for me."

She pulls out a small yellow scroll of kelpaper and hands it to Quince.

Yellow kelpaper for an urgent message.

"Simply call a messenger gull and give it this," she explains. "I will help in any way I can."

Quince thanks her, and she gives him a quick hug. I give her a longer hug. I'm not sure how much help she can be when the tests begin, but I'm glad to have her on our side.

After we say good-bye, Quince turns to me. "Call a

messenger gull?" he asks with a laugh. "How am I supposed to do that?"

"I'll teach you," I say, leaning forward to give him a quick, reassuring kiss. "It's easy."

He turns his attention to the map on the table. "You're going somewhere?"

I'm not sure if he's dismissing the trial as insignificant or trying not to think about it. I'm definitely in the second category.

"Yes," I say, relieved to be talking about the other big concern in my life right now. "I'm going to visit the kingdoms in the region."

I give him a quick rundown of my plan, how I need to gather information about the scope of the problem so I can garner support—in writing—for a joint effort to address the environmental concerns in the oceans and the mer world. So the kingdoms don't feel like they have to face it all alone.

"Sounds like a great plan," he says.

"I think so too," I reply. "I'm just not sure how to start. Calliope thinks I should talk to the nearest kingdoms first, get as many on board as quickly as possible."

"But Doe thinks you should start at the top and work down from there."

"Exactly." I stare helplessly at the map. After going around in circles with Doe's, Calliope's, and occasionally Shannen's input, I feel completely lost.

"What if the top dog won't play?" he asks.

I look up, wondering what he means.

"What if you go all the way up to the ice kingdom," he says, tracing the journey along the east coast, up to Glacialis, "and the queen says no?"

"That would be terrible," I say. "It would be so much harder to get other rulers to cooperate after that. She is highly respected."

And a little feared. I saw her power firsthand in the council meeting. She left, and the others followed. Few would actively go against her if she took a stand opposing my plan.

"What if one or two of the little dogs say no?" He draws a big circle with his finger, encompassing the kingdoms nearest Thalassinia. "What happens then?"

I shrug, beginning to see his point. "If some of them say no, then it will be disappointing."

"But not devastating?" Quince twists his mouth and shrugs at me, as if to say "Then that's where you should start."

"Plus," I continue, feeling like I am finally coming to a decision, "it will be easier to convince the smaller, less powerful kingdoms to join in the effort because they are the least equipped to deal with the problems. They should *want* to cooperate more."

"Sounds like you know what you need to do, then," he says.

I nod, grabbing the wax pencil that has rolled to the edge of the map.

"I'll start here," I say, drawing a red circle around Trigonum, Desfleurelle, and Antillenes—Thalassinia and Acropora's nearest neighbors. "With luck and a current boost from Daddy's trident, I can get to all three kingdoms this weekend."

If I can harness my new power, that will speed up the trip even more.

Quince leans in over the map, studying, and I think he's going to ask me something about the kingdoms or my plan or Daddy's trident.

Instead, without taking his eyes off the map, he asks, "What happens if I fail?"

"What?" I whisper.

"If I don't pass the three tests," he says. "What's the consequence?"

I suck in a shaky breath. This is the part I didn't want to talk about, the part I hoped he wouldn't ask about. But I guess he's too clever—or has learned too much about how mer-world magic works—to assume there won't be a price.

There is, and it's a big one.

"If you fail," I say, keeping my voice steady, "then you are banished from the water forever."

He lifts his Caribbean-blue eyes to stare into mine. "And?"

"And?" I echo.

"I know that can't be it," he says. "Nothing in your world is ever that simple."

A part of my heart breaks when he calls it *my* world. I want it to feel like his world, too. But now isn't the time. He's right; there's more to the consequence of failure than him being exiled.

"And . . . ," I say, wishing I didn't have to tell him this, "I'll be banished from land." I swallow hard. "Forever."

He stares into my eyes, unblinking, and I can't read any sort of reaction. His mind is racing, I'm sure, but everything on the outside is a stone facade.

Finally, after what feels like an eternity, he says, "Then I won't fail."

Just like that. He won't fail. He sounds as sure as he did when he first told me he loved me. No room for doubt, like he's stated undeniable fact.

I smile and act like that's all the assurance I need, but as I lean into him and let his strong arms wrap around me, I can't shake the niggle of fear. The three tests are supposed to be near impossible, even for a human who has spent a lot of time in the ocean. I have no idea how a human with little swimming ability and nothing more than the power to breathe water is going to succeed at three of the toughest challenges the mer world has ever devised.

For now, though, I need to stay positive. I have to believe that everything will work out, because the thought of never stepping on land again—of never seeing or touching Quince again—is too unbearable to even imagine.

I slip my arms around his waist and hug him tight. I won't let him go, not now that we've finally figured everything out. No matter what happens, I'll find a way to make it work.

9

I smile into the wind as Quince races us to the beach after school on Friday. Below my helmet, the frizzy length of my hair whips against my back, and I know it's getting churned into unbrushable tangles. I don't care. Soon I'll be in the water and the bird's nest will smooth out into silken yellow strands.

Quince turns his head and shouts, "I think you like this, princess."

In response I squeeze my arms tighter around his waist. I might be a complete failure at driving a motorcycle, but I've gotten pretty good at holding on for the ride.

When he slows down to turn into the beach parking lot, I sigh. The worst part of our motorcycle rides is when they're over.

He steers into a spot at the far end, beneath the shade of a clump of trees, and kills the engine. When he starts to climb off, I hold him in place, resting my cheek against the soft leather of his jacket.

Soon summer will be here, and it will be too warm for him to wear his total biker look. He'll spend the hot, humid months working construction jobs in T-shirts and work boots. Hopefully he'll still break out his biker boots for date nights.

"Not that I'm complaining," he says, wrapping his arms over mine, "but I thought you were in a hurry."

"I am." I sigh again but make no move to get up.

"But what?" He leans to the side and twists so he can see my face. "Are you worried? Nervous about going to Tri . . . ?"

"Trigonum," I finish.

I give him a kind of half nod, half shrug. I'm not sure *what* I feel. I climb off the motorcycle and, when Quince does the same, start walking to the sand.

"This is all new to me," I explain. "Except for last week's disastrous council of kings and queens, everything else I've ever done as royal duty has been in Daddy's shadow."

Quince takes my hand as we reach the beach. "So last time was a disaster," he says, and I scowl. "But you learned something, you bounced back, and you have a new plan. That's what leadership is. Learning, reevaluating, and redirecting. Everyone from the construction manager at a job site to the president of the United States has to do that on a daily basis. You're doing everything right."

"I hope so," I say. "A lot is riding on—"

Squawk, squawk, squawk!

A seagull swoops in from nowhere, screeching and flapping its broad wings wildly.

"Whoa!" Quince shouts, ducking away from the crazy bird and pulling me down with him.

The bird stops squawking and drops awkwardly to the ground. Once on the sand, it shakes out one wing and preens its beak through the disturbed feathers before pulling itself into standard seagull pose. It steps up to Quince, holds out its left leg, and waits.

"They aren't all this dangerous, are they?" Quince eyes the bird warily.

"No, but some of them are . . . a little eccentric," I explain. I glance at the kelpaper scroll, and my heart sinks. "You need to take that paper off his leg."

"How do you know it's for me?" Quince asks.

"Because he's standing in front of you. Because the kelpaper is blue, which means it's from the palace." I release Quince so he can kneel down to gull level. "And because you're expecting notification of your first test."

Quince throws me an inscrutable look before reaching out to unwrap the kelpaper from the bird's leg. As soon as the paper is clear, the gull spreads his wings, smacks Quince in the face with two big flaps, and takes off over the ocean.

Quince spits a feather out of his mouth as he unrolls the scroll.

"What does it say?" I ask.

He looks at me. "Am I allowed to tell you?"

I nod. "You can tell me. I just can't help you."

He clears his throat. "'Make your way to Thalassinia.'"

I wait for him to continue, expecting it to say that he'll receive the rest of his challenge when he gets there. But he stops.

"What else?" I say, leaning over him to read the instructions.

But there aren't any more. It only tells him to go to Thalassinia.

"Quince," I begin, but he's already shrugging out of his leather jacket and walking back to his bike.

I hurry after him.

"What are you doing?"

"Well, princess," he says as he unlocks the storage compartment on his bike, "it looks like I'm swimming to Thalassinia."

I stand there and stare for a full five seconds, watching as he stuffs first his jacket and then his T-shirt into the bike. When he starts stepping out of his boots, I jolt back into action.

"You can't," I insist, rushing forward and trying to stop him from bending down to pick up his boots. "Do you know how far away Thalassinia is?"

"A ways." He winks at me.

"Is this a joke?" I shriek, partly at him and partly at

whoever dreamed up this stupid test. "You can't seriously think you can swim all the way to my kingdom. It's forty-five miles."

Quince jams his boots into the storage compartment, then turns to face me, hands out. "Give me your stuff. Looks like I won't be taking it home after all."

He's losing his mind. "Quince," I say, keeping my words slow and steady, "you can't swim to Thalassinia. You barely learned how to swim a few weeks ago. It's too far, it's too dangerous."

He places his hands on my shoulders, and I can see that he is serious and steady. "I don't have a choice."

You do! I want to scream. But I know that neither of us wants the alternative. He wants me to be able to walk on land just as much as I want him to be able to swim under the sea. So, as much as it terrifies me to think about it, he's right. He doesn't have a choice.

"What about your mom?" I ask. Beneath my shorts, I manifest a finkini bottom. "Do you need to let her know?"

As I step out of my shorts and hand them to him, along with my flip-flops, he laughs. "Seriously? By now she's pretty much given up on the idea that my life is on a regular schedule," he says, adding my clothes to the bike before locking the compartment. "She won't start worrying until I'm gone a week at least."

I have to admire how well he's taking this. For a guy who couldn't swim two months ago, he's pretty confident. Even swim star Brody would balk at the idea of swimming that far in open water.

I take his hand in mine as we walk toward the surf. The feel of the sand squishing beneath my feet usually makes me happy, but today it only makes me nervous.

"Do you even know how to get there?" I ask.

"It's east," he says. "I think I can manage east."

He holds up his wrist, showing off his fancy sports watch—a Christmas present from his deadbeat dad. As if a watch makes up for a decade of being gone.

At least it has a compass. That'll be some help.

"It's east until you get to that rock formation that looks like a stack of Oreo cookies." I may not be allowed to help him with the physical swim, but I'm not going to let him head out into the middle of the Atlantic with no directions. "Then turn southeast. Follow the ridge line of those mountains—"

"You mean those hills?"

I growl at him. As if now is the time for a geographical debate. "That'll lead you straight to the plateau overlooking the core settlement of the kingdom. The palace is in the center."

"I've got it, princess." He winks at me again, and I want to shove him back onto the sand for not taking this seriously enough.

Instead, I finish my instructions. "If you get lost or tired or in any kind of trouble, you call a messenger gull like I showed you. Send a message to Daddy or to Peri, and they'll help you."

"I'll be fine."

"Promise me," I insist. "Promise me you'll call for help if you get into trouble."

He leans down and presses a soft, warm kiss on my mouth. I don't realize I'm trembling until he wraps his arms around me.

"I promise," he says. "Now you make me a promise."

"What's that?"

"You get your business done," he says. "Focus on your task at hand, and don't worry about me."

"But—"

"Promise." He rubs his hands up my back one more time before stepping away. "Meet me in the palace kitchen for sushi when you're done."

"You hate sushi."

He shrugs. "It's growing on me."

We both turn at the sound of splashing at the surf's edge. A single royal guard is stepping out of the water onto the beach. After the last time, I made them promise to only send one guard above the surface to fetch me. The whole squadron is too conspicuous. And embarrassing.

"Looks like your ride's here," Quince teases.

"You be careful," I tell him. "And remember—"

"I'll call for help if I need it." He drops a quick kiss on

my nose. "I won't need it. You go rally the environmental troops."

I nod and then turn to walk with my guard into the waves. As we sink under the surface, I find the rest of the school waiting just beyond the pier.

"Lily!"

Peri swims out from behind the guards.

"Peri?" I ask, confused. "What are you doing here?"

As she floats up to me, she says, "I applied to be your emissary. King Whelk interviewed me and gave me the position—mostly because he thought it's what you would want."

"Of course it is!" I squeal, giving her a quick hug.

Peri grins. "He sent me to accompany you on your royal visits this weekend." She holds up a thick folder of kelpaper. "I've been doing my research all week."

"That's great!" I'm instantly relieved to know that Peri will be at my side. I'm glad to know I won't be traveling alone. My guards are nice enough, but they're not exactly chatty.

Tellin is meeting me in Trigonum to help. Knowing I'll have both him and Peri with me is reassuring.

"Hold on a second," I tell her. "I have to take care of something before we leave."

She nods, and I swim over to my guards.

Quince may have a bunch of manly confidence in his ability to swim all the way to Thalassinia, and I believe in him

101

about a lot of things—but he is a novice swimmer. That's like a person who just ran his first mile deciding to compete in a marathon. Only with sharks and deadly jellyfish in the way, to make things more interesting. Well, I don't care what the rules say. I'm not letting him set out on his own.

"Which two of you are the best swimmers?" I ask as I approach.

They look startled, but eventually two of them raise their hands. One has bright blond hair, almost the color of mine, and the other squid-ink black. They are both young and strong and look like they could swim around the world if they had to. They'll do.

"What are your names?" I ask.

"Phyllos, Princess," the blond one answers.

The other says, "Triakis."

"In a short while, a human boy with *aqua respire*—"

"You mean Master Quince, Princess?" Phyllos asks.

What was I thinking? Of course they know who he is.

"Yes," I continue. "In a short time, Master Quince is going to enter the sea and begin making his way to Thalassinia."

"Is this the first test?" Triakis asks. "The Trial of Truth?"

I nod. Apparently the whole kingdom knows about the Trial of Truth, too. I shouldn't be surprised. Well, then there will be all the more people to celebrate when Quince succeeds.

"When he does, I want you to follow him." I take a deep breath and hope that this isn't breaking the rules, knowing that I would still do it if it was. "Don't get too close, don't interfere unless he is in danger, but make sure he is safe."

The two swimmers glance at each other and then back at me.

"We will, Princess," Phyllos says.

Triakis adds, "We will protect him with our lives."

I hope it doesn't come to that, but I am relieved to know he will be protected. He won't like it if he finds out I put bodyguards on his tail, but if everything goes smoothly, he will never know.

"Thank you."

The pair swims over to the last pylon of the pier and take up a position. They'll be able to see Quince enter the water and then follow after him. He will be kept safe. I can keep my promise to him and get on with my royal business.

"Now," I say, turning to Peri and the remaining six guards, "let's get moving. I want to be in Trigonum before sunset."

The guards surround me as they did last time, only with Peri in the center with me, and we head out toward Thalassinia's northern neighbor. Hopefully, both Quince's first test and my first royal visit will be equally successful.

10

*T*he royal kingdom of Trigonum is Thalassinia's nearest neighbor to the north, covering an area of the Atlantic bounded by the coast of the United States in the west, from Georgia to New York, and to Bermuda in the east. Along the North American coast, the kingdom is colorful and full of underwater life. In the waters far from the shore, the seas are dark, barren, and prone to storms and whirlpools. The eastern edge of Trigonum is rumored to be cursed, with a reputation for objects—human and mer alike—disappearing into what the human world knows as the Bermuda Triangle.

In the mer world we call it the Trigonum Vortex.

Thankfully, the palace is in the western part of the kingdom, off the coast of North Carolina. As we swim north, the waters get chillier. My mer powers kick in and automatically warm the water around me, but I can still feel the cold.

I can't imagine what the trip to Glacialis will feel like.

"I scoured the palace records all week," Peri says. "I made a list of important facts about King Bostrych and Trigonum so I can give you an official briefing." Peri doesn't look up from her stack of kelpapers. I smile, glad to see her so excited about this job. There isn't a merperson in all the seven seas I'd rather have at my side.

"Good idea," I reply. "The more I know, the better."

She nods absently, flipping through her papers. "I'll stick to the facts most relevant to our visit."

She finds the paper she's looking for and skims over it.

"It's worth noting," she says, "that beach erosion and potential oil and gas drilling operations are the primary threats to the Trigonum ecosystem."

"Beach erosion," I repeat, "and drilling operations."

"Human tourism is also a major concern in this kingdom," she continues. "As are commercial fishing and water pollution."

I try to keep a mental tally, but it seems like the list of problems is very long. And this is just one of ten kingdoms. I have a feeling my surveys are going to be quite full.

"But maybe the most important, though tragic, fact," she says, looking up from her notes, "is the death of the king's son last fall."

"Oh no," I cry. "What happened?"

"Prince Cirren was a scientist," she explains. "He was leading a research expedition to the Trigonum Vortex when a flash whirlpool appeared and wiped out the entire expedition."

"That's terrible." I can't imagine the impact of such a tragedy on the king. He must have been devastated. "Are those kinds of incidents common in Trigonum?"

"They aren't unheard of," Peri answers. "That's how the Trigonum Vortex got its reputation. But supposedly they are happening more frequently. And with greater intensity."

The waters of Thalassinia are relatively calm. Other than the occasional hurricane that churns the surface but leaves the depths undisturbed, we don't have many natural disasters. It must be stressful to live somewhere where they happen all the time.

"That information helps a lot, Peri," I say as we continue our northerly swim. "I'm sure it will help to go in knowing some of what's going on."

She swims close to my side. "I thought so." She tucks the folder of kelpaper notes into the messenger bag slung across her body. "I'm glad I could help."

I take her hand.

"It definitely helps to have my best friend at my side."

We swim along in silence, and I let my attention drift to the world around me. Everything is quite still. There are few fish in the stream of the faster-than-usual current. I glance up. I can see far above, just beneath the surface, the hulls of several boats. From this distance I can't tell if they

are pleasure boats or commercial fishing boats or even scientific expeditions.

As I watch, something splashes into the water next to
one of the boats ahead of us. A trail of bubbles spirals down,
falling just in front of the lead guard as we pass. I crane my
head down to see where the object lands, and when it does,
I'm appalled to see that it's a glass bottle.

"Gross," Peri says, seeing the same thing.

I shake my head. "Why would anyone think they can use
the ocean as a trash can?"

"Some people just don't think about it all," she says.

Sad but true.

Even sadder, as we swim by, I see the seaweed forest
along the ocean floor littered with all kinds of human trash.
Shopping bags, tangled-up fishing line, even a big, bright-
blue plastic barrel. It's awful.

"This is where we change course, Princess," Captain
Frater says. He makes a quick hand gesture, and the school
of guards turns as one and sets a course to the east.

We've kept pretty near the shore until now, for more
than two hours. With the magical boost to the Gulf Stream
from Daddy's trident—just one of the royal powers that
comes with being king—the complete journey only takes us
a little over three hours. We're swimming to a stop in front
of the palace before I know it.

Peri takes her position as emissary very seriously and

insists on being the one to officially announce our presence. She swims up to the front, which looks to the human eye like an abandoned shipwreck, and clangs the bell on the stern of the ship. Within moments, a pair of uniformed guards, wearing the dark teal and gray colors of Trigonum, slide open a hidden steel door.

"Who calls?" one of them asks.

"Crown Princess Waterlily of Thalassinia," Peri replies. "She seeks an audience with the king."

The two guards, twins, look at me and nod.

"Please come in, Princess," one says. "Prince Tellin is waiting for you."

The other adds, "We will notify King Bostrych immediately."

"Thank you," I say, trying to sound regal. "Please tell his highness it is a matter of some urgency."

"Yes, Princess."

With that, they leave us in the entry hall as they go to inform the king. Tellin and a single pair of Acroporan guards are waiting there, too.

"Are you ready?" Tellin asks with a nervous smile.

The message I sent him, asking him to meet me here today, outlined the basics of my plan. He knows what we're asking for and what the next steps are.

"Absolutely," I say, more confidently than I feel.

"His Highness King Bostrych of Trigonum," one of the twin guards announces as they both swim back into the hall, "invites you and your contingent to dine with him in the formal dining chamber."

My *contingent* and I follow them into the palace. I'm in the lead, with a guard on either side. Then Peri between another pair, and Tellin between his. Finally, my last two guards bring up the rear. We're quite a parade.

We pass through the halls of the shipwreck, narrow passageways lined with saltwater-preserved wood and rusted hardware. Eventually we pass through a large opening—like a giant hole in the side of the ship—and into a more merlike structure. Carved from rock and reef, the heart of the Trigonum palace is not so different from my home in Thalassinia. Rounded halls and spiraling ramps. Pearl-crusted frames around mosaic portraits. But where everything in Thalassinia sparkles with gold and gems, the details here are more modest. It is apparent that Trigonum does not possess the wealth my kingdom does.

I'm lucky to have been born into Thalassinia. I only hope I can help Trigonum in some small way and that I can convince them to help us in return.

The guards stop in front of an open doorway and gesture us inside. There, at the head of a long black table, sits King Bostrych. When he sees me enter, his round, bearded face cracks into a broad smile.

He has always reminded me of an old-time sea pirate. Tall and broad, with a round face and a big, bushy black beard. But always with a ready smile.

Several other members of his household, his family and maybe some key staff, are seated around the table.

"Oho, Princess Waterlily, Prince Tellin," he calls out with a laugh. "Please, come in and join us. The feast is just about to begin."

As if on cue, a trio of wait staff swims in with big dome-covered trays. They each take a position at the table and, in perfect synchronization, set down their trays and pull off the domes with a flourish.

Each tray is filled with a bounty of fruits and vegetables, both sea grown and from land trading.

I sense my guards staring eagerly at the offering. They are probably starving after the trip to Seaview and then the swim here. As much as I don't want to impose, it's lucky we arrived at dinnertime.

"Thank you, King Bostrych," I say, smiling and nodding. "We appreciate your generosity."

"Posh," he says, waving off my gratitude. "I doubt you swam all this way for dinner service. Come, sit at my side and let us discuss your purpose here."

Peri stays next to me as the Thalassinian and Acroporan guards take some of the open seats and quickly dig into the fresh feast before them. I nod at Peri, indicating she should join in as well—she must be just as hungry as the guards. But she shakes her head and comes with me as I swim nervously to the head of the table and take the seat to Bostrych's right. Tellin takes the seat to his left.

"Don't be nervous, Princess," he says as I sink into the chair. "I won't be holding the events of the council meeting against you. Say your piece, and I will listen with an open mind."

I take a deep breath, clasp my hands tightly together in my lap, and begin.

"As you know, King Bostrych, I am concerned about the effects of ocean warming on the people and the kingdom of Acropora."

He nods at Tellin and then reaches out to grab a handful of sea grapes. "Made that clear at the council."

Tellin blushes, and I'm pretty sure I turn bright red too.

King Bostrych pops a sea grape into his mouth and bites down. I take it as a good sign that he's still smiling and hasn't ordered me out of the room.

"Yes, well, after that meeting I realized that the problem is much bigger than Acropora." I fidget with the hem of my tank top. "The environmental issues are affecting all the mer kingdoms in different ways."

"True enough," he says after swallowing the sea grape. "We have our own problems here, to be sure."

"I know," I say, jumping on the opportunity to use some of the facts Peri told me earlier. "You have beach erosion and commercial fishing and oil and gas deposits that humans are just waiting to drill."

"You've done your research, then?"

My cheeks burn. I won't take credit for Peri's work. "I've

had help, your highness."

"That's all well and good," he says, pulling a big fat eggplant onto his plate. "But that still don't explain why you're here."

I reach behind me, holding out my hand, and smile when I feel the waxy curl of kelpaper.

"I'm here for two reasons, your highness," I say, setting the survey and the petition Peri just handed me onto the table. "First, I want to create a detailed list of all the environmental challenges facing Trigonum."

"Have you got a year?" King Bostrych asks with a humorless laugh.

"I know, it's a lot," I say. "But we can't start to fix the problems until we know what they are."

"I suspect that's fair to say." He pops another sea grape into his mouth and nods. "What's the second reason?"

"We want to form an alliance," Tellin explains.

My hands shake as I spread the papers on the table to reveal the petition. "An interkingdom commission on environmental concerns."

King Bostrych looks downs at the papers with curiosity.

"What does this commission entail?" He looks up at me, and I see wariness in his dark-gray eyes. "Trigonum ain't the richest kingdom in the sea. We don't have sacks of treasure to throw around—"

"Oh no, no, no," I interrupt. It's rude, but I don't want him to think I want money from him. "For today, all we want is your pledge of support. For you to say that you're concerned about what's happening in the oceans—in your kingdom and in others—and that you're interested in figuring out a way to change things. Together."

I hand him the petition so he can read the pledge for himself. Shannen helped me with the wording, so I know it sounds impressive.

"And *after* today?" he asks. "Signing a paper won't do a lick to clear the pollution from our waters."

"No, your highness, it won't," I reply.

"This is only the first step," Tellin explains. "Once the commission is in place, it will become active. Part of its purpose will be to organize relief efforts. Then we get a protocol in place to call for aid from all the kingdoms of the Western Atlantic when disaster strikes, so that help comes faster and from more sources."

"The other thing we will do," I add, "is create what my friend Shannen calls a resource matrix."

"Resource matrix?" King Bostrych repeats.

"It basically means we'll look at what resources each kingdom has," I say.

Tellin adds, "And what they need."

"Then we can create a circle of aid." I draw my finger in a circle on the table. "Maybe you need cloth, but you have a surplus of crab this year. Thalassinia will send you a sea truckload of cloth, while you give a portion of your crab harvest to Rosmarus. Then Rosmarus gives Thalassinia a delivery of swordfish, and the circle is complete."

"Sounds complicated," King Bostrych says.

I thought the same thing when Shannen first suggested it. But the more she explained it, the more sense it made.

"It kind of is," I agree. "But once it's in place, it will just be a matter of staying organized. Besides," I say, giving him an earnest look, "I think it's worth the effort, don't you?"

He studies me, and I see the concern in his eyes. He's worried about his people. The situation in his kingdom might not be as bad as Acropora's—yet—but it could be heading that way.

If he would just see that our only hope for solving this massive problem is to work together.

"It surely is," he says, answering my question as his wariness fades into a smile. "Where do I sign?"

I reach back again, and Peri slips a pen into my hand. I hand it to the king. "Right at the top."

With a flourish, he signs the first line under the petition.

We, the undersigned kings and queens of the Western Atlantic, do hereby indicate our interest in the formation of an interkingdom commission on oceanic environmental concerns and how to address them, with the understanding that this commission will seek to streamline disaster relief and improve trading of essential resources.

Bostrych, King of Trigonum

As he hands the pen and the petition back to me, I heave a huge sigh of relief. Now that my nerves are settling, I realize that I'm as famished as my guards. As the wait staff brings out another set of trays—this one with a rainbow display of fresh-caught sushi—I am relieved that this first stop on my royal trip is going so smoothly.

I give the signed petition to Peri, and she slides it into her bag as she finally takes a seat at the table. She and Tellin both dig into the sushi.

"Now," I say to King Bostrych as I place a few pieces of sushi on my own plate, "we know about *some* of the environmental problems facing your kingdom. Tell me about the *rest* of them."

ith yet another survey complete and another signature added to my petition, I swim away from my meeting with King Zostero of Desfleurelle feeling confident about my plan. With his pledge of support today and one from Queen Cypraea of Antillenes yesterday, that makes three names on my list, and three surveys full of environmental concerns.

Antillenes, which is located in the southern Caribbean, is suffering a lot of the same problems as Acropora: warming waters, dying coral, and diminishing food supply. Desfleurelle, on the other hand, is suffering different problems in the Gulf of Mexico, many of which are caused by human drilling operations.

It's daunting to think of everything that we need to work on, but at least the rulers are being receptive to cooperation.

"This is going well," I say to Tellin. "Don't you think?"

When he doesn't respond, I turn to look at him. He looks lost in thought, like his mind is somewhere else. As I focus on him, the connection of our bond slams me with sadness. The feeling is so strong, I almost start to cry.

If I hadn't been so focused on my mission, maybe I would have noticed earlier. But I guess I must have blocked out the connection.

"Tellin," I say softly, laying a hand on his shoulder.

He looks up, startled, and stops swimming.

I drift to a stop with him, and around us Peri and the guards stop too.

"What?" He shakes his head. "Sorry, I was . . . thinking."

"I can see that," I say. "And I know you're thinking about something sad. Want to talk about it?"

His eyes widen for a second, and then he nods, as if remembering the bond and the reason I can sense the mood of his thoughts.

"I'm just thinking about home," he says, shaking his head. "When I left my father, he was . . . not in a good place. He is sick and dying and angry."

"That's understandable," I say. "I can't imagine what you're going through."

I don't remember my mom—at all—so it's hard to even miss her, really. It's more like I miss the idea of her. Even that is really hard sometimes.

But the thought of losing someone I know and care about, of watching him get sicker and weaker, knowing what's going to happen and that there's nothing to do about it? Well, it's no wonder Tellin is sad and distracted.

"You should go home," I tell him. "We're done with the kingdom visits for this weekend. There's no reason you should swim all the way back to Thalassinia before heading south."

"Are you certain?"

"Absolutely." I place my hands on his shoulders, sending as much positivity and assurance I can through our bond. "I'll send you a message when I know where we're starting next weekend."

I sense him wanting to argue, but in the end his emotion wins out. "Okay," he says. "You're sure you can get home safe?"

"Of course." I gesture at the half-dozen guards in Thalassinian uniforms. "We have half an army to protect us."

Tellin grins and pulls me into a grateful hug. "You are a true pearl."

I give him a quick squeeze and then shove him away. "Get going," I say. "You have farther to swim than I do."

Tellin waves to his Acroporan guards and starts off in a more southeasterly direction. They will hug the coasts of Cuba and Haiti before rounding the tip of the Dominican Republic and heading due south to the palace. My little parade, on the other hand, just has to swim through the Florida Keys and then northeast to Thalassinia.

"Come on, guys," I say to my guards as I take Peri's hand. "Let's go home."

We haven't gone fifty yards when someone swims out from behind a large rock formation to our left and blocks the path. The guards quickly tighten around me and Peri in a defensive circle. Each guard draws a Thalassinian dagger, a three-bladed knife that looks like a really sharp, handheld trident, and aims it at the intruder.

"P-p-princess Waterlily?" the girl stammers.

Through the wall of mer shoulders, I peer out at the great threat. She's a small slip of a mergirl, not more than thirteen or fourteen, I would guess. Her long hair, so black it's almost midnight blue, swirls around her in the current.

Her hands, clutched over her heart, are shaking in fear.

"Stop, you're terrifying her," I say to the guards. I place my hands on the shoulders of the two directly in front of me and propel myself over their mer-made wall.

Peri follows close behind.

"No, Princess," Captain Frater shouts as I kick myself toward the girl.

Her tailfin is breathtaking. Scales in iridescent shades ranging from bright green to midnight blue. It looks like a giant peacock feather.

"I am Princess Waterlily," I tell her, swimming closer.

Her wide-eyed gaze stares over my shoulder.

"My guards are putting their weapons away now," I say, throwing a meaningful scowl over my shoulder in case they miss the fact that that's an order.

I watch until they reluctantly resheathe their blades.

Then I turn back to the girl.

"What's your name?" I ask.

"Aurita," she replies, her voice barely a whisper.

"It's very nice to meet you, Aurita," I say, extending my hand to her.

She takes my hand and shakes it gingerly, her own hand still shaking. She doesn't let go.

I wonder why she's waiting for me beyond the royal city of Desfleurelle. I don't want to push her, though. She's already terrified, and it might scare her off if I start asking questions.

I just smile and wait for her to talk. Eventually she does.

"Is it true, Princess," she asks, "that you live on land?"

Ah, maybe she is considering a life on land and wants to know what it's like. I'm more than happy to answer those questions.

I smile at her. "Yes, I do."

"And that you love a human boy?" she asks, almost right on top of my answer.

"Yes." My smile grows bigger. Maybe she's a romantic. Or maybe she has her eye on a human boy of her own. "His name is Quince and—"

"Princess, he's in danger," she blurts.

"What?" My voice rises to a squeak, and I sense the guards close in behind me at my cry of alarm. Peri floats closer to my side. I try to calm myself enough to find out more. "What do you mean, he's in danger?"

Despite the extra precautions of royal guards, being a mer princess is not usually a dangerous job. Not in Thalassinia, anyway. There has never been an assassination attempt in my kingdom, and those in other kingdoms have been few and far between.

It never once crossed my mind that my position might put Quince in danger. I'm not sure I could live with myself if he got hurt because of me.

"Not just him," she explains, and my anxiety levels drop a little. "All humans."

That's not much better, but at least it's not a specific threat against Quince.

"Please explain, Aurita." I take the girl's hands in mine, trying to calm her down. "Why are humans in danger?"

"My king," she says, "King Zostero. He is angry at humans for treating the oceans so poorly. He wants revenge for the oil spills and the pollution."

"Revenge how?" I ask, not liking the sound of this at all.

Her eyes, the same blue-green shade as her tailfin, dart around like she's afraid of being overheard.

I lower my head close to hers. "You can whisper it to me," I say softly. "No one else can hear you."

I wave Peri away, and she swims back over to the guards.

With a nod, Aurita stretches up and places her mouth right next to my ear. "He plans sabotage," she breathes. "He wants to destroy human technology so they can't destroy our world anymore."

I lean back and try to process this accusation. I just left King Zostero's chamber, where he seemed more than happy to join my efforts to help the mer world recover from its environmental problems. I hadn't sensed any underlying anger that might indicate his thirst for revenge. Then again, I had been pretty focused on my mission and on giving my speech about cooperation and the strength of a united front.

I want to question her, but without its looking like I doubt her accusation.

"Why are you telling me?" I ask. "I mean, why tell anyone? You don't agree with your king?"

Not that I agree with him, but I'm pretty sure most of the mer world blames humans—all humans—for the current state of the oceans. While I don't think the matter of blame is that simple, I also know that *we* haven't been polluting our oceans or drilling for oil in the seafloor. I don't hold humans individually accountable for the problems, but humankind as a whole is definitely the cause of a lot of the mer world's problems.

That Aurita is speaking out against her king, and to a foreign royal no less, indicates that something more is going on here.

"My brother," she says, her blue-green eyes starting to sparkle, "my half-brother is human. He does not know about me, our mother, or our world, but he works on an oil platform on the northern edge of our kingdom."

She bites her lip, like she's overcome by emotion.

"The king plans to sabotage the drilling platforms." She shakes her head. "I am afraid my brother will be hurt or killed when this happens. The king does not care if humans die. He only cares about revenge."

From what I've heard about offshore drilling platforms, the whole thing is crazy dangerous. If the king sabotages the equipment, it's entirely possible that someone will die. And it will look like an accident.

My hands shake and I clench my jaw.

My first instinct is to turn around and swim back to the palace. I'd like to give King Zostero a piece of my mind about revenge not being the answer and something about guilt by association.

But that doesn't seem like the smartest course of action. If Aurita's accusations are true, he's already upset and acting on emotion. Now *I'm* upset, and just as emotional. Bringing the two of us face-to-face right now is probably a recipe for disaster. I don't want to accidentally put Thalassinia and Desfleurelle at war over something that can be handled more . . . diplomatically.

"Thank you for telling me this, Aurita," I say to the girl. "It was very brave of you to come forward."

She smiles through her tears. "I knew you were the only one who would understand. You know what it means to care for a human."

"I do." And more than one. I care just as much about Aunt Rachel and Shannen as I do about Quince. And now that Brody is bonded to Doe, he's pretty much family too. Yes, I'm probably the best merperson to understand this problem.

"I am going to figure out how to stop this," I say. "I'm going to talk to my father, the king, and we will find a solution."

"Thank you," she says, and bows her head.

"I may need to get in touch with you again," I say. "Where can I send a messenger gull?"

"To the palace," she replies.

"The palace?" I echo, a bad feeling knotting in my stomach.

"Yes," she says sadly. "I am King Zostero's youngest daughter."

Then, before I can react, she turns and swims away. I watch as her beautiful peacock tailfin flashes away into the deep.

Great—this just got even more complicated. I have a feeling Daddy and I are going to have a long discussion about this.

I swim back over to my guards and exchange a worried look with Peri. As soon as we're clear of Desfleurelle waters, I'll tell her what Aurita said. Then, as soon as we get home, I'll tell Daddy. We'll figure out what to do.

At least Quince will be waiting for me when I get there. For the first time, I'm glad he has to go through these tests. Instead of wishing I was home in Seaview, we'll be sharing some tasty sushi in the palace kitchen. Knowing he's there will make the journey home go so much faster. My concern for his safety resurfaces, and I'm even more eager to hurry home and wrap my arms around him.

"Okay, guys," I say to the guards. "Let's really go home this time. I'm exhausted, and I think I have a long night ahead of me."

$\mathcal{A}$s I swim into the palace alone—the guards stopped at the gate to give a report to their commander, and Peri headed home—the palace housekeeper, Margarite, greets me at the front door.

"Welcome, Princess," she says, giving me a deep bow.

I want to roll my eyes at the unnecessary ceremony, but I don't have the energy. I just want to find Quince and sushi and then talk to Daddy about everything I've learned so I can sleep for at least ten hours.

"Hello, Margarite," I say. "Is Quince waiting for me in the kitchen?"

Her dark brows pinch into a puzzled expression. "Master Quince? He is not in the palace."

"What?" My heart thumps, and a jolt of adrenaline enters my bloodstream. Not even the calming effects of the sea can soften my reaction. "He should be here by now. He—Where is my father?"

"In his office, Princess," she says, her eyes filled with sympathy. "I believe he is awaiting your arrival."

I don't wait to hear the rest of whatever she's saying. I take off as fast as my kicks—and an extra push of current from my new power—can carry me, racing through the halls toward Daddy's office.

Quince left Seaview almost two full days ago. Even with his weak swimming skills, he should have gotten here sometime yesterday.

Images of everything that might have happened to him flash through my mind. Shark attack. Riptide. Ship propeller. Stronger-than-usual Gulf Stream current. He could have been swept all the way to Glacialis by now.

By the time I swim through Daddy's door, my vision is blurry and I'm sure my teary eyes are sparkling like flecks of gold. My breath comes in short, fast gasps.

"Lily," Daddy says as I enter, "I've been—"

He freezes midsentence when he sees the look on my face.

"Quince," I blurt. "He's supposed to be here. The first test. He's been swimming for two days. We have to go find him!"

Daddy darts quickly from behind his desk and wraps me in a tight hug. "Mangrove," he calls out to his secretary, "call

127

the chief of the guard. We need to send out a search party."

"He should be here by now," I sob against Daddy's chest. "What if he—what if—"

"Shh." Daddy rubs a hand up and down my back. "I'm certain he is fine. He is a strong young man."

"But he can't swim." I pull back and give Daddy a pleading look. "I mean, just barely. He's been learning, but still, he only started a few—"

"We will find him," Daddy says with such certainty that I want to believe him.

His assurance calms me enough to start thinking clearly. Daddy's right, Quince is strong. Between my directions and his compass watch, he had to stay on the right path. Besides, he wasn't alone.

"I sent two guards with him," I say. "They would have protected him if anything came up."

Daddy's face turns stony. Blank. "You sent guards?"

"Yes," I explain. "I had more than enough to spare, and I wanted them to watch him. Just in case. Why, is that a problem?"

He hesitates, thinking, before shaking his head. "It's fine." He turns, one arm still around my shoulders, and we start for the door. "Let's go find Quince."

Mangrove returns from alerting the chief of the guard just as we reach the hall. "The search party awaits you at the palace entrance, your highness."

"Thank you," Daddy says as we swim by. "Please find

Calliope Ebbsworth as well. She will need to be present when we return."

I take off out of the palace faster than I've ever swum before. My exhaustion from a weekend of traveling disappears, and all I can think about is getting to Quince. And trying *not* to think about all the millions of awful things that might have happened.

My path is clear in my mind. I know Quince will have followed my directions, so I start them in reverse. As I swim northwest out of the city, my guards can barely keep up with me.

I hear them calling out to me.

"Princess!"

"Wait for us!"

"Don't swim out of sight."

Daddy and his entourage are far behind.

I ignore them all.

Kicking harder, I sweep over the suburbs, leaving behind the outer edges of the city. The landscape fades into more natural shapes, those that haven't been molded by mer hands to form houses and restaurants and grocery stores. Here there are only sea creatures, marine plants, and the rock and sand that they inhabit.

In my rush to crest the hill that overlooks Thalassinia, I crash into the trio of bodies on the other side.

"Oooof!"

"Ow," I say, grabbing my head. Something hard—like an

elbow, maybe—has connected with my skull, and for a few seconds my vision is blocked by bright spots.

Then I hear it.

"Lily?"

Quince's voice is weak.

I squeeze my eyes shut a few times to clear the spots, and when I open them again I see Quince floating right in front of me.

"Quince!" I shout, diving against him and wrapping him in the tightest hug I think I've ever given. "Holy bananafish, I was so worried about you."

His arms hug me back, but not as tight as usual. "I was a bit worried about me, too."

He says it in his usual joking manner, but there is a tension in his tone that I've never heard before. I lean away, then—seeing the dark circles under his bloodshot eyes—I float back far enough to take all of him in.

Besides his tired-looking face, his whole body looks wrung out. His arms hang limp at his sides, his legs drooping below. His shoulders, usually broad and straight and strong enough to carry a blue whale on his back for a few miles, sag with a weariness I've never seen in Quince.

I swim forward and smack him in the shoulder. Hard.

"You promised!" I smack him again. "You said you would call for help if you were in trouble."

When I go to smack him again, he grabs my wrist and pulls it to his chest. "Wasn't in trouble. Just . . . slow."

"It's been two days," I say, trying to keep the screeching panic out of my voice. *"Two days."*

"Has it?" His dark-blond brows pinch into a scowl. "Kinda lost track."

I shake my head at him. Then, turning to the two guards I sent to protect him—cowering a few feet away, next to a giant sea fan—I say, "I told you to protect him. To help him."

Phyllos raises his hands in surrender. "We tried, Princess. When we realized he had only made it halfway in a day, we revealed ourselves and offered to help."

"He refused," Triakis adds. "Said he had to do this on his own or it didn't count."

"We're going to have a conversation about you sending babysitters after me," Quince says. "Later, when I can feel my legs again."

I scowl at him and then the guards, but I can't exactly blame them. Mostly because Quince is right. He has to do this test alone, without help, or he'll fail. And then we'll both suffer.

"Just tell me I'm close," Quince says to me. "That'll give me the second wind to cross the finish line."

"You are," I answer quickly. "Not far at all."

"Ah, I see you've found him," Daddy says as he arrives on the scene.

"He's exhausted," I tell Daddy, "but he's determined to finish."

Daddy nods. "Then the least we can do is escort the lad the rest of the way."

"Are you sure that won't break the rules?" I ask. "I don't want him to have gone to all this effort just to throw it away."

"It's fine," Daddy insists. "So long as no one pulls him home."

I give Daddy a grateful smile before turning to Quince.

"Okay, let's finish this thing," I say. "We'll swim at your pace and I'll be by your side the rest of the way."

He smiles. Not quite the cocky, mischievous smile I've grown to know and love, but that guy is in there, under the exhaustion.

Quince tilts forward and reaches out, scooping his hands back in a wide arc to propel himself forward. I notice that his legs are barely moving, like he doesn't have the energy to add a kick to the stroke.

"How can I help?" I ask, desperate to do something more than just watch him scoop his way to Thalassinia.

"Tell me a story," he says, his eyes drifting half shut. "Tell me about your weekend."

Okay, I can do that.

"Let's see," I say, trying to figure out the most interesting way to tell him about my very boring travels. For a human who hasn't visited those kingdoms, though, I suppose they're not so boring. I decide to skip the diplomatic mission parts and focus on the adventure.

"First we went to the kingdom of Trigonum. It's north of

Thalassinia, and the Bermuda Triangle is in the eastern part of the kingdom."

"Cool," he says, his pace picking up a little bit. "Do wake-makers and other mer things go missing there too? Or is it just human planes and ships?"

"A bit of both," I admit. "The vortex has been known to whip up some pretty dangerous whirlpools. I guess it's like the mer-world equivalent of tornado alley, only with whirl-pools instead of twisters."

Quince smiles, and that's all the encouragement I need to keep going.

"Because of the triangle, there are lots and lots of ship-wrecks in Trigonum," I tell him, and I feel like I'm telling a bedtime story. "Human-object salvage is one of their big-gest industries. They export things like deck chairs and fine china and even trinkets like pocket watches and jewelry."

"Pirate treasure?"

"Not as much as you'd think," I reply. "But some, defi-nitely. There's a rumor that they found a huge collection of Spanish gold coins last year, but a human salvage operation found it at almost the same time, so they can't recover the treasure."

Quince nods, and we swim in silence for a few strokes. I'm glad that my guards and Daddy and his guards are keep-ing a fair distance. That makes it feel like Quince and I are swimming home alone.

"Tell me more," he says. "Where else did you go?"

"Next I went to Antillenes, the Caribbean kingdom south of Acropora." I close my eyes and picture the beautiful blue seas, the vibrant sea life, and the friendly people who make up one of the Western Atlantic's most southern kingdoms. "That kingdom is very laid-back, even by mer standards. They are extremely rich in rare sea flowers and they have a big mer tourism trade, so they are a wealthy kingdom."

Quince doesn't respond, but he keeps swimming. So I keep talking.

"Their queen, Cypraea, is one of the most beautiful mermaids I have ever seen." Every mermaid in all the seven seas is jealous of her beauty, and I'm no exception. "She has long golden-blond hair that flows almost to the tip of her tailfin. And her scales are gold and ivory."

"Doesn't hold a candle to you," Quince whispers.

"You haven't seen her yet," I argue.

"Lily, don't—"

"Oh, look," I shout when he starts to tell me not to put myself down—which I don't need a bond to tell me he was about to do. "We're almost to the city's edge."

Quince's eyes open wide, and he smiles at the sight of Thalassinia's suburbs.

"Now you just have to make it to the palace in the center," I say, cheering him on. I think back to three years of watching Coach Hill motivate the swim team. Sometimes he just cheers for them, sometimes he tells them they're losers who couldn't beat a Chihuahua doing a dog paddle—I never really understood that one—and sometimes he tries to motivate them with rewards. I've had more pizza dinners than I can count because the boys kicked it up a notch to best their times for the promise of free food. Maybe that technique will work on Quince.

"Let's race," I say. "If you win, we can have seaghetti for dinner instead of sushi."

"And if you win?" he asks.

I give him a wicked grin. "You have to eat hoya."

"What's hoya?"

"Sea pineapple," I answer innocently.

He frowns. "That doesn't sound like a punishment. I like pineapple."

"This isn't pineapple," I say as I kick my tailfin a little harder, pushing myself into the lead. "In fact, it isn't even a plant."

The disgusted look on his face is quickly followed by faster arm strokes and even some kicking. I smile as he catches up to me, and even though I keep pace evenly with him as we cross the city—and even though I know I could beat him with one full-strength kick—I also know that when we get to the palace, he's going to *just* beat me by a blade of seagrass.

A few minutes later my prediction proves true. It's uncanny how I know these things.

13

After watching Quince gorge himself on pretty much everything the palace kitchen has to offer—even the sushi—I ask Margarite to escort him to the starfish room. He needs a good night's sleep after his two-day swim. He might need a good *week's* sleep to recover from that.

But knowing that he's catching up on his rest relaxes me as I swim toward Daddy's office. I never knew I could care about someone so much without the benefit of a bond to magnify our emotions. I can only imagine how strong our connection would be if we hadn't severed.

"Knock, knock," I call out as I swim past the guards stationed at Daddy's door. It's late, but I knew he would still be working. Still waiting to hear my report about my royal visits this weekend.

He's not going to like what he hears.

"Lily," he says, his handsome face spreading into a warm

smile. "I had a feeling you would be by again."

"Hello, Princess Waterlily."

I cringe at the sound of Calliope's voice. It's nothing personal—her voice isn't high-pitched or anything—but her presence usually comes with bad news of some sort. Hopefully this visit is just about checking in on Quince's first test.

"Calliope," I say, forcing a smile. "How are you tonight?"

"Wonderful," she replies. "King Whelk was just filling me in on the details of Quince's adventure. Sounds like it was a bit of a challenge."

"You could say that." I throw Daddy an irritated look. "You could also say he almost didn't make it."

Calliope's face falls. "I know it was difficult, but he did pull through in the end."

"I know," I say by way of apology. "I'm just really exhausted. Is there anything you need from me right now?"

"No, I don't think so." Calliope glances at Daddy, who shakes his head. She turns back to me with a sunny smile. "I think I have everything."

She gathers up her stuff and swims for the door.

"Thanks, Calliope," I say.

"Anytime," she says cheerfully.

When she's gone, I float into one of the chairs facing his desk.

"You look exhausted, daughter," he says, his voice soft with concern.

"I am," I admit, allowing my eyes to drift shut for a moment. "It's been a long weekend in a lot of ways."

"Yes," Daddy says, setting aside the papers on his desk, "and I want to hear all about your travels, but first, how is Quince?"

"Recovering," I answer, forcing my eyes open. I need to be alert and awake for this discussion. "He'll be fine. But I can't believe he had to do that, Daddy. How could you ask him to do something so dangerous?"

His face falls serious. "If I could have found a way around the test, I would have," he insists. "The law is very specific."

"He could have died," I say. "Maybe he wouldn't have drowned, not since you restored his *aqua respire*, but any number of things might have happened to him between here and Seaview."

"I know." His gentle eyes soften in what looks like genuine hurt. "And I know the pain that would have caused you, but there was no other way."

I shake my head. I've lived in the mer world all my life—even when I'm on land, I'm still part of this world—but I'm starting to realize there are things I will never understand. The ancient laws are among them.

I don't want to dwell on my anger over something that is done. Quince is safe. I can argue about ancient laws in modern times on another day. Tonight we have bigger problems to address. "We need to talk about my weekend."

"Yes," Daddy says. "Tell me about your visits. Were they successful?"

I give him a brief recap of my visits to Trigonum and Antillenes, about the results of my surveys and the agreement each ruler made to be part of a cooperative commission.

"But I learned something important in Desfleurelle," I say. "As I left the kingdom, I was stopped by Princess Aurita, who told me something terrible."

Daddy frowns. "What?"

"She said King Zostero is planning to sabotage offshore oil drilling rigs in his kingdom." I close my eyes at the thought of the potential consequences, the potential losses. "Those rigs are dangerous. If they're sabotaged—"

"Lily . . ." Daddy trails off, his voice sounding almost sympathetic. "Princess Aurita has a developed a reputation for dramatic stunts. She has become the mergirl who cried shark, I'm afraid."

"What do you mean?" I ask. "You think she's lying?"

"Last year, she called a council of kings and queens and falsely claimed an infestation of mer-hungry sharks was devouring her kingdom." Daddy shakes his head. "King Zostero revoked many of her royal privileges after that."

I picture the scared girl who stopped me on my way out of the kingdom. I may not always be the best judge of character—I thought I hated Quince for a long time—but nothing about Aurita's demeanor said she was lying or making things up.

139

"You didn't see the look in her eyes, Daddy," I say, trying to convince him. "She looked truly frightened for her brother."

"Brother?" Daddy puffs out a sad laugh. "King Zostero has only daughters."

I clench my jaw. "Her *half*-brother," I explain. "He's human and he works on one of the oil rigs and——"

"She manipulated you, Lily," he says. The pity in his tone sends a shot of lead down my spine. "She obviously knows of your love for Quince and exploited that to make you believe her."

"But——"

"She cannot call dramatic council meetings anymore," he continues, "so she is using you to bring her attention."

I fall silent, trying to process Daddy's words. He's basically accusing Aurita of lying and me of falling for it. I can't believe that. I mean, I can't believe he doesn't trust me. And I refuse to believe she was lying.

The sparkling tears in her eyes are proof enough for me.

"You're wrong," I say. I don't usually argue with Daddy—and by usually, I mean never—but I can't just sit aside and let bad things happen to innocent humans. "I believe her, and if you won't do something about it, then I will. I don't want the consequences of King Zostero's actions on my conscience."

I kick up from the chair, ready to storm out of the office in a show of rebellious certainty. But before I can swim away, Daddy says, "Lily, wait."

I stop moving, but I don't turn back around. Growing up, I never thought I would have to use Doe's tactics to get Daddy to do something. I used to roll my eyes at her pouting and storming away. But today, when the cause is so important, I can see the benefits of her methods.

Not that I will *ever* tell her that.

"If you believe so strongly," Daddy says, his tone more serious than pitying, "then I will investigate the situation."

"Investigate?" I whip back around. "We have to do more than just investigate."

"Investigation is the first step," he replies. "I cannot go in accusing the king of plotting against humans. It would put him on the defensive, whether he is guilty or not."

I take a deep breath and try to see the reason in his argument. He's right. Just rolling into a royal palace and lobbing accusations at the king is the surest way to be tossed either out the front door or into the palace jail.

"Okay," I say, forcing myself to be reasonable. "I'll go with you."

He shakes his head. "It will be better if I go alone. Besides, you have obligations on land. You have graduation in just a few weeks' time."

"That's true," I say reluctantly. "But I can miss a day of class. This is more important than my attendance record. I don't want to sit around waiting and wondering."

"That is unnecessary. I will visit Desfleurelle and then

141

send you a messenger gull with the results of my inquiry as soon as it's done."

I consider his suggestion. To be honest, the idea of turning around and swimming all the way back to Desfleurelle after my weekend of travel is a little depressing. And it's not like I don't trust Daddy to do what he says he's going to do. I know he will.

I relent. "Okay," I say, not really happy but willing to accept the situation. "But you send me that message as *soon* as you're done."

"I promise," he says with a smile. "Now I think you need to go catch up on your rest as well. You look nearly as exhausted as Quince did earlier."

A yawn I didn't know was coming pushes out, and I try to cover it with my hand.

Daddy chuckles.

"I guess you're right," I say around a second yawn that I don't try to stifle. "I could use a good night's sleep too."

I push off and start to swim out the way I almost stormed out a minute ago.

"Lily," Daddy says again, and I turn back to face him. "I am very proud of you, daughter. Whatever the results of my inquiry, your compassion and concern are wondrous traits in a princess."

"Thanks, Daddy," I say, a proud smile breaking across my face. "I'll stop in and say good-bye before we head out in the morning."

He grins, and as I swim out the door and head for my room, I know he's going to spend half the night working. Maybe someday he'll let me take over enough duties that he can take some time off.

Another yawn washes through my body, and I swim faster for my room and my bed. I don't even have the energy to change into a sleep top before my head hits the pillow.

"*P*ardon me, Princess.

A soft voice pulls me out of a nightmare about Quince drowning in an oil slick. I woke up about a dozen times in the night, shaking with fear for what might have happened to him in his first test. Needless to say, I'm happy to return to reality.

I blink my eyes open and spot the source of the voice, a timid palace maid floating a few feet away from my bed.

"Forgive the intrusion, Princess," she says, keeping her eyes averted, "but—"

"We made her do it," another—familiar—voice calls out.

I lift my head and see Peri and Quince in the doorway.

"Look what I found in the palace kitchen," Peri says, nodding at Quince. "I'm amazed there's any food left in the kingdom after the way he was devouring Laver's culinary concoctions as fast as the cook could make them."

I smile at the pair of them.

"I need the nourishment," Quince says in his defense, patting his stomach. "Do you know how many calories it takes to swim here?"

I turn to the maid, who looks like she's trying to make herself as invisible as possible in the corner of my room. I've never seen her before. "What's your name?"

"Bailya, Princess."

"Well, Bailya," I say, giving her a reassuring smile, "thank you for waking me. I am always available to these two."

I get a beaming smile in return. "Will there be anything else, Princess?"

"No, thank you," I say. "Please go on about your day."

With a grateful nod, Bailya darts across the room, around my two visitors, and out into the hall.

"Give me five seconds," I say, pushing back my covers and heading across the room. "I need to freshen up."

"How was last night?" Peri shouts to be heard inside my bathroom. "Did you tell the king about Aurita's claim?"

"Yes," I say as I grab a cloth from the shelf beneath the counter. "And you know what?"

"What?" she asks.

"He doesn't believe her," I reply. "He doesn't believe *me*."

I scrub the cloth over my face, and the action both relaxes and energizes me. I do the same at key spots—under my arms, base of my neck—and then reach for the toothpaste.

"Peri, can you bring me a clean tank?" I ask. "They're in the—"

"I know where your clothes are," she says before I can finish.

Seconds later, she's handing me a turquoise tank. She whispers, "I heard Quince had trouble with the first test. Did it turn out okay?"

I nod. I dart behind the changing curtain. "The swim from Seaview to Thalassinia nearly killed him." Stripping off my dirty tank, I open the lid on the laundry hamper and drop it inside. "I don't know how he will manage two more."

As I swim out from behind the curtain, sporting the turquoise tank, Peri grins. "He will. Because he loves you, and that's the point."

"Are you two gabbing in there?" Quince shouts. "I'm starving."

"You just ate half the pantry," Peri shouts back. She winks at me before adding, "Save some food for the rest of the kingdom."

We swim out into my room.

"Actually, I'm starving too," I say. Then, because I can't help myself, I add, "If there's any food left to eat, that is."

"Ha ha." Quince throws an arm around my shoulder as I swim by, pretending like he's going to throttle me but then changing his mind at the last second and kissing me instead.

"I thought you two were hungry. But if I'm wrong," Peri says, swimming ahead, "I'll just go ahead and eat your share."

146

Quince laughs at Peri's teasing. As he takes my hand and swims after her, I'm impressed. His swimming has improved a lot, and he's actually pulling me with him. I start kicking, just to get us moving faster, and can't help but smile.

I'm glad to see Peri and Quince getting along so well. I mean, it's not like they're going to be spending tons of time together—he may be able to breathe underwater, but he's still human—but it's nice to know my best friend and my boyfriend can hang out and have fun.

When we swim into the kitchen, I swear Laver looks at Quince and starts shaking. But he's a trouper and just orders his sous-chef to pull another order from the pantry.

Quince, Peri, and I sink onto stools at the kitchen counter and wait for breakfast.

"I'm not surprised the king doubts Aurita," Peri says, grabbing us each a glass of orange-juice gelatin from a tray on the counter. She spoons out a bite and lifts it to her mouth. "She's got kind of a reputation for stirring up controversy."

As she swallows her bite and Quince takes one of his own, I swirl my spoon through the gelatin. "So I've heard," I say. "But you saw how scared she was. You saw her hands shaking and her eyes sparkling."

"Maybe she's a really good actress," Peri suggests.

"What are you two talking about?" Quince asks, looking up from his juice.

"When we were in Desfleurelle," I explain, "the mer kingdom in the Gulf of Mexico, we learned about a plan to sabotage human enterprises."

Quince frowns. "Like what?" he asks.

"Like sabotaging offshore oil rigs."

Quince whistles—pretty impressive under water. "That's dangerous."

"I know. But Daddy doesn't believe me." I shove my gelatin away. "Because of the source."

"So he's not going to do anything?" Quince asks.

"No, he is," I reply. "He's going to visit King Zostero to ask him about the rumor."

Laver sets a tray of gourmet breakfast sushi in front of us, and Quince quickly stabs at an awabi roll with his seasticks. The jab comes a little too close for Laver's comfort, and he jerks his hand away before it winds up skewered.

"And then what?" Quince asks before popping the sushi into his mouth and, I swear, swallowing it whole.

I shrug, making my own selection from the tray. "Then we wait and see. He's going to send me a message as soon as he has an answer."

"King Whelk will do the right thing," Peri says, obviously sensing my divided emotions. "He will find out what's going on and will act accordingly."

"I know," I say. "I trust Daddy."

I'm just not sure if I trust him more than my own instincts. Everything inside me screams that Aurita isn't lying. Aunt Rachel always says I should trust my gut, and my gut is telling me that King Zostero is planning something.

"We'll see what Daddy finds out," I say, mostly to Quince. "Then I'll decide what to do."

"Um, Princess?"

I turn at the sound of a quiet voice, half expecting to see another timid palace maid.

I nearly drift off my stool when I see Astria floating there, with a respectful look on her face, and the lower half of her red hair dyed the same mint-green shade as her tailfin. I bite back a smile. Peri chokes on a laugh. Quince goes back to his second breakfast.

"Excuse the interruption," Astria says, flicking her gaze at Peri and Quince, "but may I speak to you in private?"

I'm so stunned by her seemingly genuine respect—that's a first—that I can't answer.

Peri responds for me.

"Anything you have to say to Lily," she says, her amusement at Astria's hair now forgotten, "you can say in front of us."

I lean back instinctively, braced for Astria's wrath. She does *not* like to be put in her place.

So when she merely takes a breath and says, "Please, it will only take a moment," I'm stunned.

"Um, sure," I say, giving Peri a wide-eyed what-the-frog-is-going-on-here? look.

Peri shrugs. Yeah, I don't have a clue either.

Equally curious and afraid this is some sort of humiliation master plot, I follow Astria into the hall outside the kitchen. When she turns to face me, she can't look me in the eye. I'm starting to lean more toward the master-plot option.

"What you said to me the other night," she begins, "about the problems in our world and the pettiness of gossip . . ."

Oh no, she's going to totally light into me. I tense, ready to flee.

"I haven't been able to stop thinking about it, and . . ."

I float back a few inches.

"You're right."

I stop kicking and just stare at her.

"What?" I ask as my momentum knocks me into the wall. I push away, floating back to Astria. "What do you mean?"

"I mean you're right," she says. "There are things happening in our world, and I want to help."

I think my brain just imploded a little. First Doe stops being a wicked brat, and now Astria wants to help. Surely these are signs of a looming apocalypse.

"Um, okay?" I half say, half ask. I feel so off-kilter, I don't even know which one I'm doing.

"If you need anything," she says, finally looking me in the eye, "anything at all, just ask."

She floats forward and presses a slip of kelpaper into my palm.

"This is my address. Send a gull or a message bubble anytime, and I will do whatever I can to help your efforts."

I think I nod. Or maybe I just stare, slack-jawed, as she turns and swims away. I don't think my brain can process what happened.

When I swim back into the kitchen, Laver is setting out another tray of food for Quince. Peri looks up, relieved.

"What did she want?"

"I . . ." I shake my head as I float back onto my stool. "She wants to help."

"She what?" Peri asks.

"Really?" Quince mumbles around a bite of sea-fan toast.

"Yeah," I say. "She . . . I guess she finally realized there's something bigger at stake than making other people feel bad."

Peri scowls. "I still don't trust her."

I shrug. I don't know, maybe I'm the worst judge of character in history, but I think she was being sincere. As we all go back to eating our breakfast—Quince is on his third or fourth, at least—my mind is racing through everything that happened this weekend. Quince's test. My royal visits. The sabotage plans. And now Daddy's investigation of Aurita's claim.

I want to figure out what to do next, but the truth is I can't decide anything until Daddy talks to King Zostero and sends me his message. Quince and I need to get back to Seaview and get on with our days.

The message will come in time.

Hopefully, answers will come with it.

15

"*J*t's good to be a senior," Brody says, leaning back against the picnic table.

"And a sophomore." Doe pokes him in the ribs.

Brody grins at her. "But sophomores aren't supposed to eat lunch outside. That's a senior's right."

"It's true," Shannen says, carefully unwrapping her sandwich.

Doe sticks out her tongue. The old Doe would have huffed and stormed away, but the new Doe just smiles and peels her orange.

I take a bite of my apple and lean into Quince's side.

We all agreed to bring our lunches today so we could ditch the cafeteria for a little time in the sun. I'm trying not to get tense every time a seagull flies by. Waiting for Daddy's message is making me nuts. I'm sure it won't come until at least after school, what with the time required for him to travel to Desfleurelle, speak with the king, and then send word to me.

Plus I'm still exhausted from all my swimming this weekend. Maybe I could catch a quick nap. I drop my head onto Quince's shoulder, glad that he decided to ditch the leather jacket in the heat, because that means there's only a thin layer of tee between him and me.

My eyes are closed and I'm just about to drift into dreamland when a loud voice says, "Hi, Brody."

My shoulders tense.

"Hey, Court," Brody says.

I sit up straight. Brody's ex-girlfriend is not my favorite human on the planet. When I had a crush on Brody, she was pretty horrid to me. I brace myself for whatever she's about to say.

To my utter shock, she turns and saunters over to the next picnic table and sits down with her friends. Is that going to be the end of it? She didn't even say a word to Doe.

Then it happens.

"I mean, seriously." Courtney's voice floats over to our table. "Who carries a briefcase to high school?"

Every eye at our table locks onto Doe, whose briefcase is at her feet.

She meticulously peels the rest of her orange, pulls the segments apart, and sets them on her napkin. Gathering up the peel, she stands.

"I'll be right back."

We all watch as she walks over to the nearest trash can. I think I'm holding my breath as she drops the orange rind into the garbage and turns back around. She's walking so casually, I think she's going to let it go.

Then, right as she passes the other table, she stops and leans down to whisper in Courtney's ear.

Courtney's spine stiffens. She turns and gives Doe a confused look. Doe nods.

I wait for the return fire, for Courtney to throw out some terrible comment in response to whatever Doe just said.

Instead, she nods in return and then turns back to her lunch.

Quince, Shannen, and I exchange stunned looks. We've all seen the wraths of Doe and Courtney individually. I think we all expected there to be fireworks when they finally confronted each other. This was . . . kind of anticlimactic.

Doe walks back to our table and takes her seat. I don't miss the fact that she reaches under the table to take Brody's hand. I'm amazed by her transformation. Clearly, being with Brody has been good for her.

"What did you say to her?" Shannen asks.

Doe blinks innocently as she says, "I told her if she ever spoke to my boyfriend again, I would send the entire school a picture of her American Girl–themed bedroom."

Brody shrugs. "I thought it was cute."

"I don't know what that is," Doe finishes. "But I understand it is quite embarrassing."

We all burst out laughing at Doe's brilliant blackmail. Leave it to my cousin to figure out how to take on Courtney once and for all.

We finish our lunch in peace and sun worship until the bell rings.

As we are walking back inside, I hear the familiar squawk of a messenger gull. I glance in the direction of the sound and spot it sitting on a hibiscus bush outside a row of classroom windows.

"I'll meet you inside," I tell my friends as I drop and pretend to tie my shoelace. "Cover for me."

Shannen nods and hurries inside. As soon as the doors close behind them and the picnic area is empty, I stand and walk over to the bush. After a quick peek into the window to make sure there isn't a class inside, I approach the gull.

I do one more quick glance around and then reach forward. The gull holds up its foot to give me better access. I quickly untie the string securing the kelpaper to its leg and remove the scroll.

"Thank you."

The bird screeches and then flaps its wings, soaring into the sky and toward the ocean.

"Lily?"

I jump at the sound of my name. Spinning, I see Miss Molina standing on the sidewalk near the door I was supposed to have walked through to return from lunch.

"Oh, hi," I say, quickly shoving the kelpaper into the

pocket of my shorts. "I was just, uh, looking at this hibiscus flower." I reach for the nearest flower, a bright white bloom. "Isn't it awesome?"

Miss Molina crosses the grass between us, and I think she's going to inspect the flower. Instead, she asks, "Did you just take something off a seagull's leg?"

My heart pounds like crazy. "Um, what? No, that's—"

"I saw you." She nods at the windows behind the bush. "That's my classroom. I was at my desk and watched as you walked up to the bird, untied something from its leg, and took off a piece of paper."

Oh no, oh no, oh no.

Think, Lily, think. I have to come up with a believable explanation. One that doesn't involve mindwashing Miss Molina, because this definitely isn't a disastrous enough reason to give myself a migraine. Surely I can come up with—

"Is it a pet?" she asks. "I've heard that seagulls can be trained, but I always doubted their reliability."

"Yes!" I practically shout, grateful for her giving me an answer. "My aunt Rachel trained him to bring me messages at school." I pull the crumpled kelpaper out of my pocket and hold it up as evidence. "Isn't that cool?"

"Very." She turns her head in the direction the bird went, like she's hoping to spot it in the sky. When she doesn't, she turns back to me. "Very impressive." Then, as if remembering that I'm a student and not in class, she says, "Shouldn't you be somewhere?"

"Yes," I say. "Art. Don't want to be late."

Miss Molina smiles as she says, "Then you'd better be on your way. The second bell is going to ring soon."

I nod and start around her, heading for the door. I'm two steps onto the sidewalk when I turn back.

"Can I ask you something?"

She smiles and joins me on the sidewalk. "Of course."

"So, you remember how I asked you about getting people involved in an organization?" I ask, twisting the kelpaper of Daddy's scroll in my hands.

Miss Molina nods.

"Well, what if some of the people involved want to do things a different way?" I ask, trying to word this in the most generic, there's-nothing-weird-about-me, I'm-not-a-mermaid way possible. "What if they want to do something I think is wrong? Or illegal?"

"That sounds very dangerous, Lily," she says, her tone and her face equally serious. "Maybe those people should not be involved in your organization."

Like that's an option.

"What if they have to be?" I ask. "How do you convince people that what they're doing is wrong?"

"You could go to the police," she suggests.

I bite my lips so I don't laugh. There is no such thing as

police in the mer world, only royal guards and the judgment of kings and queens. And telling human police is so not an option.

"What if I can't?" I ask, and from the confused and concerned look on her face, I can tell she's starting to worry about me. Maybe this was a bad idea. Maybe I'm worrying about nothing and Daddy's note says there's no truth to Aurita's claim. "I'll figure it out," I say, turning to leave, eager to get inside and read the message. "Thanks anyway."

"Why are they doing it?" she asks. When I turn back around, she adds, "Do they believe they are doing these things for the right reasons?"

I think about it for a few seconds and then sigh. "Yes, they do."

"You know, when I was in school, I was involved in a group dedicated to saving the Everglades from tourism and development." She gives me a small smile. "Some of the other members thought we needed to achieve our ends by any means necessary. Some of them went so far as burning a small cruise boat that took tourists through the swamp."

"Oh no," I gasp, covering my mouth with my hand. "Was anyone hurt?"

"Fortunately not," she says. "But those involved were arrested, and our organization fell apart in the face of the scandal."

"That's terrible."

"The saddest thing was," she says, "they thought they

were doing the right thing. Or at least for the right reasons. Their lives, as well as the life of the tour operator and the relations between the people who make a living from the swamp and the environmentalists who want to preserve it, were irreparably damaged."

This is exactly what I'm afraid of happening in my world. If there are merfolk determined to sabotage human operations in the seas, then that will affect both worlds in a bad way.

"To this day," Miss Molina continues, "I regret not doing something to stop them. If you are facing a similar situation, my advice is to find another way for your friends to achieve their end goals. You can't stop them head-on—I tried that. You need to find an alternative solution."

That's what I'm trying to do. I'm trying to get the mer kingdoms to work together instead of taking on these environmental challenges on their own, mer against human.

I guess it's good to know that I'm doing the right thing. I'm not even sure that anything needs to be done. I might just be overreacting, wanting to believe Aurita because I don't want to be wrong. I hope that's the case, because the idea of merfolk fighting humans leaves my stomach in knots.

The bell rings and I'm going to be tardy. Again. At least my art teacher, Mrs. Ferraro, isn't really strict about that.

"Thanks, Miss Molina," I say, backing away to the door. "That helps a lot."

"You're welcome," she calls out as I run inside.

My heart pounds as I unroll the scroll, eager to see what Daddy found out.

FROM THE DESK OF

KING WHELK OF THALASSINIA

After discussing the matter with King Zostero, I believe
I was correct. Princess Aurita fabricated the tale and there
are no such sabotage plans in place.
   Sorry.

   Daddy

I reread the words three times. This can't be right. I was *so* certain that Aurita was telling the truth. *So* certain.

But Daddy wouldn't lie—he has no reason to—and I trust his judgment. If he says she was making it up, then she must have been making it up.

I crumple the kelpaper in my fist.

Just because I accept his answer doesn't mean I like it. I don't like being wrong, and I don't like the idea that Aurita totally played me.

As I hurry to my locker, I tell myself I was wrong about Aurita. Everything is going to be fine, and next weekend I'll do my next round of royal visits to get support for my plan.

Everything is going to work out.

* * *

160

"I thought your father said there was nothing to the sabotage rumors," Quince says as he stomps into my kitchen a few mornings later. His biker boots clomp across the floor, rattling my breakfast dishes.

He slams the morning paper down on the table and says, "Explain this."

Prithi meows at the noise intrusion and dashes from the room.

Confused, I scan the front page headline.

TWO WORKERS MISSING AFTER OIL RIG ACCIDENT

"Oh no," I gasp.

I skim the article, which talks about an unexplained accident at an offshore oil rig in the gulf—along the northern edge of Desfleurelle. A piece of machinery that was inspected only last week malfunctioned, sending two workers overboard and several to the infirmary. This is exactly the kind of thing Aurita warned me would happen.

"I thought your dad said there was nothing to worry about," Quince says. "I thought he checked things out."

"He did," I insist. "He thought Aurita made it all up."

"Clearly he was wrong."

"This could just be a coincidence?" I suggest weakly. I don't like thinking that Daddy made this kind of mistake and people got hurt.

Quince scowls at me. "Lily . . ."

"I know, I know," I say. "He was wrong."

He was wrong to trust King Zostero over Princess

Aurita, and I was wrong to trust Daddy's investigation over my gut. I knew something was going to happen, I believed Aurita, so the responsibility lies with me.

The article says that while search efforts continue for the missing workers, the rig is out of commission due to the malfunction. King Zostero wanted revenge, wanted the drilling to stop, and he succeeded. I only hope that Aurita's brother isn't one of the missing or injured men.

Now my responsibility is to make sure nothing more happens to endanger human lives.

I walk to the still-open kitchen door and call a messenger gull. While I'm waiting for it to arrive, I grab a sheet of kelpaper and a squid-ink pen from the junk drawer and scribble a note.

> *Daddy,*
>> *You were wrong. Please send guards to accompany me to Desfleurelle after school today. I will leave from Seaview Beach Park at 4:00 p.m.*
>>> *XOXO,*
>>> *Lily*

When the messenger gull is on its way, I turn back to Quince.

"I can't undo what happened," I say. "But I can try to stop it from happening again."

He crosses the room and wraps me in a hug.

"I know you'll do your best."

"Geez, can't you two keep your hands off each other for five seconds?" Doe snarks as she walks into the kitchen.

"You're one to talk," I throw back. "You and Brody are practically glued at the hip every time I see you together."

She shrugs as she pulls open the fridge. "That's different. We're cute."

If I had something other than Quince within reach, I'd throw it at her.

She flashes me her I'm-so-cute-and-innocent smile before taking a sip of grape juice. "So what was all the stomping and grumbling?" she asks. "Did Lily scratch your motor-cycle again?"

"Again?" Quince growls.

"Doe!" I might throw Quince at her after all. I step away from him. "Really, it wasn't a scratch. More of a smudge. Um, dust. Really."

For a second he looks angry, but then he just shakes it off. To Doe he says, "There was an offshore drilling accident last night. Looks like the merfolk are starting their revenge."

Doe's eyes widen, and she looks stunned into silence—a first. She turns to me. "What revenge? What is he talking about?"

I guess I haven't seen her much since I got back. Like I said, she and Brody are inseparable, and I've been pretty busy.

After I give her the bullet points, she says, "Aurita's a trip, for sure, but she wouldn't lie about something like this."

"I guess we've learned that lesson now," I say.

"What are you going to do?" she asks.

I'm surprised that she sounds genuinely concerned. Except for her somewhat misguided attempt to make me keep my title for the sake of the kingdom, Doe doesn't take much notice of royal affairs. And until recently—as in *very* recently—she would have applauded these efforts of revenge against humans. She hated all humans with a pretty violent passion, blaming them for her parents' deaths. Now that she loves Brody and has been spending time with humans—him, Aunt Rachel, and Shannen—she's definitely more human friendly.

"I'm going back to Desfleurelle tonight," I reply. "To try to talk some sense into King Zostero."

Doe nods, like she approves of my plan. Then she shocks the seaweed out of me by saying, "I'll come with you."

"What?" I shake my head. "No, you don't need to do that."

She flips her caramel-blond hair over her shoulder in a careless gesture. "I know. But I *can* and I *want* to."

I exchange a look with Quince, and he shrugs. He's always believed that there is a smart, caring, *mature* mergirl somewhere inside Doe—somewhere deep, *deep* inside. Maybe he thinks this is a sign that her maturity is surfacing.

Maybe it is.

"Okay," I say. "Meet me in the parking lot after school.

We'll head straight to the beach."

As if nothing major just happened, Doe sets her glass in the sink and flounces out of the kitchen, her knee-length skirt swinging with every bouncy step.

"What just happened?" I ask. "I mean, was that my cousin *volunteering* for something? Again?"

"Sure looked like it." Quince smiles. "Want me to give you two a ride to the beach? I can borrow my mom's car."

"No," I say, my mind still on Doe volunteering to join me. "I'll take my car. Who knows when we'll be getting back?"

Quince is silent for a second before asking, "Did you really put a scratch on Princess?"

"Um . . . no?"

Quince lifts one dark-blond eyebrow above his piercing Caribbean-blue eyes. Like he can stare me into a confession.

Okay, maybe he can.

"It's teeny-tiny," I say, backing toward the kitchen door. "You can't even see it unless you're really looking and—"

I turn and run upstairs, acting like I need to escape before he freaks out. Instead, I just hear his laughter roaring through the house. Maybe the idea of a scratch on his baby made him go insane.

I hide at the top of the stairs, waiting for him to catch me. When he does, I gladly accept my punishment in the form of a big, hard kiss.

When he pulls away, I'm breathing heavily.

"You know you're going to give her a bath," Quince says.

"A bath?"

He rests his forehead against mine. "And scrub her until your *smudge* is gone and her body gleams."

"Okay," I sigh, leaning into him. "I'll totally do that."

He winks. "And I'll totally sit back and watch."

I close my eyes and wait for even more punishment.

I don't have to wait for long.

16

*W*hen Doe, Brody, and I arrive at the beach that afternoon, the first person to emerge from the water is Daddy. The look on his face—sad and serious, with deep wrinkles of concern etched on his forehead—tells me that he feels every ounce of his mistake. There's no point in rubbing it in.

A pair of his guards walks out behind him. Not that I don't love my guards, but his are so much more intimidating. Even a great white would turn tail and swim the other way.

"What are you doing here?" I ask.

"I will escort you to Desfleurelle," he says. "Zostero lied to my face, and I will not stand for that."

Daddy's arms and shoulders are tense. *He's* tense. His fists are clenched at his sides. Bad sign.

"I'm not sure that's such a good idea," I say. "We don't

need to start a war over this. That won't help things."

"I won't send you alone," he says. "If Zostero is willing to lie to me and attack humans, I don't trust him with you."

"I won't be alone," I say quickly. "Doe's coming with me."

"Aurita and I have a history," she tells Daddy, hugging her arm around Brody's waist.

"Ah yes," he says, a scowl forming. "I remember."

"We're over that rivalry thing," she says. "Well, at least I am. I think I can help."

"Lily," Daddy says, turning back to me, "I don't like the idea of you—"

I step forward and lay my hands on his shoulders. This is the moment when I go from being Daddy's protected little girl to Princess Waterlily, who puts duty first.

"Trust me," I say. "I was right about Aurita, and I'm right about this. This is my cause."

He takes a deep breath and then releases it. "Yes, you were right. If either of those missing men is dead, I won't—"

"We didn't make this happen," I say, trying to reassure him. "King Zostero did. Now I want to do my best to make sure it's the last time."

Daddy nods, relenting.

"You will take a double school of guards," he says. "And I will have more at the ready. You need only send a message bubble, and the entire Thalassinian guard will be at your side."

"I really don't think that will be necessary," I reply with

a nervous laugh. At least I *hope* that won't be necessary. "I'm just going to talk to him. Reason with him, you know."

"I will trust your judgment in this," he says. Then, turning to Doe, he adds, "And I am glad you will be there as well."

He turns and walks back into the sea, shouting, "Be careful," over his shoulder as he goes.

Next to me, Doe is practically glowing. As the perpetual black fish, wild child in the family, she's not used to such a compliment. She's not used to people trusting her. Which probably only ever made it less likely for her to do something worth complimenting.

"Time for me to go, baby," she says to Brody.

"You're sure you don't want me to come with?" he asks.

She leans up on her toes and gives him a kiss.

"I'm sure." She drops back down and sets her hands on his hips. "Besides, this is one of the last times you'll be able to stay when I go. After the new moon next weekend, we'll be eternally tied to each other."

Brody gets that swoony look on his face, and I decide it's time to break up the mushfest.

"Come on, Doe," I say as I start walking down the beach. "Let's go."

I don't watch as she says good-bye to Brody, and then she's next to me and we're almost to the water.

"You keep volunteering for stuff like this. . . ." I drape an arm over her shoulder and squeeze. "Next thing you know

169

Daddy will be appointing you Thalassinian ambassador to Nephropida."

"Ew, no thank you," Doe says, shrugging off my arm. She blushes, like she's uncomfortable with the idea of such responsibility. Then, in true Doe fashion, she says, "Maybe Costa Solara. I could use some work on my tan, and I hear the shelf off the coast of Belize is just breathtaking."

"Deal," I say, laughing at her oceanista attitude.

Then the time for teasing is over, and we're walking into the water, heading out into the ocean and around the horn of Florida, then making our way on speedy currents to the Desfleurelle palace. As we travel, I realize I don't have much of a plan. But I guess I don't need one. I just want to talk to the king, to try and explain that sabotage isn't the answer. Maybe he'll listen and maybe he won't, and later I'll figure out the next step. But for today, I just want to talk.

That doesn't stop my heart from beating a crazy pattern as Doe and I wait outside the royal chamber for an audience with the king.

"You need to relax," she says.

"I know," I say, resisting the urge to say duh. "I don't think I'll ever get used to speaking with kings and queens."

"Well, you'd better," she says. "Your future holds kind of a lot of that."

This time I give in to the urge. "Duh."

Knowing and accepting are two different things.

"His majesty will see you now."

I take a deep breath and, with Doe at my side, swim inside. The king is sitting behind his desk, looking a lot like Daddy when he's working. Except where Daddy's hair is salt-and-pepper gray, King Zostero's is still inky black. Like Aurita's.

"Princess Waterlily," he says with an overdone smile, "I did not expect to see you again so soon. And Lady Dosinia . . ." His eyes narrow. "Such a pleasure."

"Mutual," Doe says.

"I think you know why we're here, your highness," I say. If I keep my tone respectful, maybe things will go better. Smoother. "I was right about the sabotage, and the oil rig accident was your first attack."

"Ridiculous. I cannot be held accountable for human mishaps." His smile falls away. "What I wish to know, Princess, is where you got this false information."

"That doesn't matter—"

"Aurita," Doe says.

"Doe!" I gasp.

"Trust me," she mutters. Then, to the king, "Your daughter entrusted Lily with the truth, and she was right to do so."

King Zostero studies Doe for a minute, maybe trying to gauge her angle in the situation. The old Doe would definitely be doing this for some kind of benefit, but the new Doe . . . I think she actually has a plan.

"My daughter has been prone to exaggeration in the past," he says to Doe.

171

"So have I," she replies. "But not anymore. Aurita and I have both done some growing up. She wouldn't exaggerate, not about this."

Doe meets his gaze head-on, and for a minute it feels like I'm a spectator at a staredown, waiting to see who blinks first. Zostero may be a mer king, but my money's on Doe outlasting him. She has nerves of steel.

"You are correct," he finally says, breaking eye contact and turning to face me. "My daughter was not lying."

"Well . . ." I hadn't expected such an easy admission of guilt. Now what?

"I do not regret my actions, past, present, or future. Did you really expect to stop me?" he asks. "Either of you? You may not approve of my methods, but the end results will speak for themselves."

"What end results?" I demand. "What do you expect to win by injuring and killing humans?"

"I wish to scare them out of our waters," he says. "When they suffer enough losses—whether of life or money—they will retreat. Our oceans will be our own again."

"That's . . ." I shake my head. I want to say it's crazy, but this is exactly what Miss Molina was talking about. Like her old friends from the Everglades, he's doing wrong things—he even knows they're wrong—but he thinks he's doing them for the right reasons. Telling him he's wrong isn't going to magically fix things.

But maybe telling him his expectations are wrong will.

"You won't scare them away," I say. "A few accidents, even a few lives lost"—I shudder—"in the gulf won't force them out of the oceans altogether. At best, it will drive them to another corner of the seas."

His dark eyes watch me carefully as he says, "Not if the attacks occur in more than one kingdom."

He says it so gently, with so much certainty, I almost miss the meaning.

"Wait, what?" He can't mean what I think he means. "Are you saying . . . ?"

"There are other kingdoms involved," Doe fills in. "How many?"

He shrugs carelessly. "Several."

"Several!" I can't believe this. "How did you get several other kingdoms to agree to this terrible plan?"

He shrugs again and sits back, crossing his arms over his chest. How can he act so nonchalant about this? About endangering human lives?

I kick forward and lean across the table.

"Your highness, why did you do this?"

Doe floats up next to me. "*He* didn't."

I turn to her. "What do you mean?"

"Desfleurelle is not a terribly influential kingdom in the Western Atlantic," she says, giving him an appraising look. "King Zostero couldn't gather a family of sea cucumbers to his side, let alone a group of powerful rulers. Not on his own."

"But someone else could," I say, realizing what Doe

means. "Who? Who is helping you?" I want to smack the smug look off his face, but I know that won't help. Besides, solving violence with violence never works. That's what *he's* trying to do.

"Who?" I demand again.

"You will find out in time," he says. "Now, if you ladies will see yourselves out, I need to go speak with my daughter."

Oh no. Aurita is going to be punished because Doe revealed her as our source. I flash her a fearful look.

As we swim out of the royal chamber, she whispers, "Don't worry about it. I sent her a message bubble as soon as we reached the edge of the kingdom. She'll be waiting for us outside the palace gate."

I am in awe. Doe was amazing in there. She knew exactly what to say and how to play Zostero to get him to confess. I'm so glad she came with me.

"Doe, I . . ." Not knowing what other words to use, I simply say, "Thank you."

"Don't go getting used to this," she says, winking at a cute guard as we leave the castle. "I'll be back to being your bratty baby cousin in the morning."

"Even if you are," I say, though I have my doubts about that, "I'll love you anyway."

I don't miss the blush or the hint of sparkle in her eye as she kicks ahead of me. Yep, it looks like a more mature Dosinia has arrived. And just when I need her the most.

$\mathcal{D}$ oe and I make fast time for home after sending Aurita to the Thalassinian royal palace with half of our guards and a note for Daddy, telling him what has happened and asking him to house and protect the now-outcast princess. The sun is just starting to rise in the east.

As we swim up to Seaview Beach Park, I'm stunned to see a school of royal guards entering the water. I exchange a look with Doe, and she shrugs, just as confused as I am.

"What's going on?" I ask, floating over to the nearest guard. "Are you looking for me?"

The guard jumps a little at my approach, startled. Then, recovering himself, he says, "No, Princess. We were sent to fetch Master Quince back for his second test."

"What?"

I swim past the guard and, with a powerful kick, launch myself out of the water. I land on the sand, fin changed into a finkini bottom, and scan the area for Quince. He's in the corner of the parking lot, stripping off his shirt and storing it in his motorcycle.

"What's going on?" I ask, running over to him.

"Princess." He grins, and the way his eyes crinkle at the corners wakes up butterflies in my stomach. "I was wondering if you would make it back in time."

Forcing the butterflies to calm down, I ask, "You got another messenger gull?"

Quince nods. "Right in the middle of breakfast. Freaked the heck out of my mom." He lowers his gaze. "You know, someday we're going to have to tell her the truth about you."

"I know. Someday. What did the message say?" I probe. "What is your second test?"

"No clue." He shuts the storage compartment on his bike, and we start walking down the beach. "Just said to come to the palace for the second test." He reaches into a cargo pocket and pulls out the kelpaper. I read, hoping for another clue, but it says no more than that.

"At least I don't have to swim there on my own this time," he says. "Your boys in blue are giving me a ride."

"Forget that," I say. "*I'm* giving you a ride."

"Ditching me already?" Doe asks, but I can't tell if she's teasing. "And just when we were starting to get along."

"I have to go with him, Doe," I say. She should understand; I know she'd do the same for Brody. "I can't let him—"

"Joking, cousin," she says, dismissing my explanations. "Give me your keys so I can get home."

"My keys?" I balk. I've only had my car for a couple of weeks. I've only barely learned how to drive it. Does she really think I'm going to let her take it for a spin?

"Relax," she says, holding out her hand. "Brody's been giving me lessons."

"But it's a standard," I argue. "It's really tricky to manage the clutch and the brake and—"

"Brody's Camaro is a standard," she replies. "Trust me, I've got this."

I take a few deep breaths and stare her down, daring her to tell me she's joking again. She doesn't. Palm up, she waits for me to give over the keys to my car.

"You're *sure* you know how to drive?"

Doe cocks her head to the side, as if she's not even going to dignify that with a response.

"Okay," I say, reluctantly dropping my keys into her outstretched palm. "But if you hit anything—"

She saunters away before I can finish my warning. I watch, eagle-eyed, as she unlocks the door, slides into the driver's seat, and brings the car to life. Seconds later, she's pulling out of the parking lot. Flawlessly.

Seriously, not a jerk or a screech or a stutter. Smooth, as if she's been driving all her life.

"She doesn't even have a license," I whine as my taillights disappear down the street.

177

"I'm sure she'll be fine," Quince says, patting me on the back.

"How does she do that?" I demand, turning on him. "She's been on land, what? Just over a month? I've been here almost four years, and she's got the human thing down like it's nothing."

"Master Quince," the lead guard says before my tirade can continue, "we really should get going."

"Yeah," I say, disgusted at Doe—and myself. "Let's go."

Once I'm back in the water, with Quince's arms wrapped tight around my waist for the swim home, my frustration ebbs. I should be happy for Doe, proud of her for fitting in so well. Especially since she plans to spend a lot of time on land with Brody in the future.

"Feel better, princess?" Quince asks as we reach the deep ocean.

I sigh. "Yes."

"You know you're good at things that make her jealous, right?"

"Like what?" I huff.

"Like making people smile." He squeezes me tighter. "You're brilliant at that."

I want to grumble—like making people *smile* is a tangible skill—but instead I grin. That's better than nothing, I suppose. And I've got bigger things to think about right now. Quince's second test, for one, and the news about the sabotage conspiracy.

We'll take care of Quince's test first. Then I can talk to Daddy about what I learned in Desfleurelle.

Quince and I swim through the palace gate, expecting the guards to lead us to the main entrance. Instead, they take us around the outside of the palace. As we round the first tower, I see Daddy, Calliope, and a few other merfolk waiting.

They are standing at the edge of a part of the royal gardens called the Night Garden.

It's one of the most breathtaking underwater gardens in Thalassinia. Because it's made up entirely of plants and animals with bioluminescent glow, on nights when there's a new moon, with no lunar light filtering down through the water, the Night Garden shines bright as the sun.

I remember watching a video about fireflies in biology. There was a part—when the narrator wasn't talking about larval form and chemical reaction—where it showed time-lapse photography of a forest when firefly glowing was at its maximum. At one point, it was like the entire forest was awash in light.

That's what the Night Garden is like.

Even in the filtered late-morning sun it's spectacular.

"Hello, Princess," Calliope calls out to me as we approach. "Quince."

I wave at her and Quince says hello.

"Lily, I am glad you are here," Daddy says when he sees

me. "I want to hear about your meeting after Quince finishes his test."

I nod. "Definitely."

"But for now," he says, "you need to stay on the sidelines with us."

"Remember," Calliope adds, "you cannot help Quince in any way."

"I understand," I reply.

"So do I," Quince says, letting go of my waist so he can swim around to my side. "I'm ready."

"You might remember I said your second test would focus on mental strength," Calliope says, leading Quince to the Night Garden path. "Well, it specifically focuses on memory."

"It will test your ability to remember sequences," Daddy explains.

"This path," Calliope says, pointing at the strip of dark gravel that weaves through the garden, "follows a circular route. Along this route are several creatures trained to glow in a chain reaction, each time adding another glow to the chain."

"In short, son," Daddy says, "you will need to watch them light up, remembering the order, and then re-create the chain by touching each creature in the same order."

"Oh, okay," Quince says, smiling and nodding. "We had a game like this growing up. If you pushed the lighted buttons in the wrong order, it blasted you with an alarm."

"With this test," Calliope says, "if you get the order wrong, you fail."

Some of the humor fades from Quince's face.

"How many chains does he have to remember?" I ask. "How many sequences?"

"The chain will begin with only one," Daddy says. "And will gradually build to sixteen."

"Sixteen?" I gasp.

Quince makes a choking sound.

"Why so many?" I ask. "Isn't that kind of . . . excessive?"

"The number sixteen was chosen for a very specific reason," Calliope says.

"Yeah," I mutter. "To make it impossible."

"Ten for the number of kingdoms in the Western Atlantic," she says, pointedly ignoring my comment. "Five for the number of original mer kingdoms. And one more for Capheira, the sea nymph who granted us our powers."

"Sixteen," I grumble.

"Don't worry, princess," Quince says. "I can do this. I *will* do this."

"Come," Daddy says as Quince swims into the garden, "we can watch together from above."

Daddy and I float up to a place where we can see the entire garden path. I'll be able to see every glow and watch every choice Quince makes. Calliope takes her position next to us, clipboard in hand and ready to judge Quince's performance.

She reaches out and pats my hair. "He'll do fine."

I smile at her. "I hope so."

I cross my fins and fingers that he succeeds.

The first few rounds go quickly. The first chain is simply a glowing anemone at the garden entrance. Quince touches the anemone, making it glow again, and then the second chain starts. First the same anemone again, and then a sea star on the other side of the circular path. When he touches those two in order, they glow again, followed by a bed of red-glowing seaweed back by the entrance.

This goes on and on. Quince easily remembers one, then two, then five glows in sequence. And the fact that each chain only builds on the last makes things easier.

When it gets up to eight, he starts to slow down. I can see his forehead scrunching as he tries to remember the last couple of links in the chain.

By twelve, he's starting to look mentally exhausted. And physically, too, since each chain requires him to swim around the garden path more and more.

At fifteen, he's barely floating from glow to glow. He's been doing this for hours now. It takes him a solid three minutes—I know, because I started counting seconds—to remember the last link.

But he finally does, and I cheer.

"Good job!" I shout. "One more to go!"

He looks up and gives me a weary smile. Then he turns

his attention back to the garden as the final chain starts glowing.

I follow the pattern with my eyes, anticipating the first several I have memorized, and then catching up with the glow of the rest. When the fifteenth glows, I scan the garden eagerly for the sixteenth and final glow in the final chain.

I wait and wait and wait and . . . nothing.

"Did I miss it?" I whisper to Daddy. "Where was the last glow?"

He holds a finger to his mouth in response.

I look at Quince, hoping he saw what I didn't, but he looks just as lost.

After studying the garden, waiting for a glow, he finally starts the last chain. I watch, nervous, as he touches the fifteen glows in order. Then, after the fifteenth, I hold my breath.

Where was the sixteenth glow? I didn't see it, and I have a clear view of the entire garden. How could Quince have seen it from down on garden level?

"There was no glow," I say to Daddy, who ignores me. "This isn't fair!" I shout down at the garden, getting Quince's attention. "The sixteenth object never—"

I gasp as Quince pushes off from the seafloor, jetting straight toward me.

"Wait, what are you doing?" I demand. "You can't just give up, you have to—"

Quince reaches me, and instead of wrapping me in a hug like I expect, he reaches for my hair. I try to swim back, away from the near-desperate look in his eyes, afraid that he's going to fail the test.

He tugs something from my hair.

I look down and see a *Padina antillarum*—a beautiful little seaweed shaped like ginkgo leaves—in his hand. And it's glowing.

"You," he says with an explosive grin. "*You* are the sixteenth object."

I look nervously at Daddy, afraid that Quince might be wrong, that maybe it's just coincidence that there's a glowing *Padina antillarum* in my hair at just the right moment—and not long after Calliope patted my head.

When Daddy nods, I release a huge sigh of relief.

Calliope winks at me, then goes back to making notes on her clipboard.

I attack Quince with a massive hug.

"You did it!" I shout, pressing kisses all over his handsome face.

"I told you I would," he says.

"I never doubted you," I reply.

He leans back and gives me a skeptical look.

"Well, not *really*."

"Congratulations," Calliope says, holding her clipboard against her chest. "Two tests successfully completed, only one more to go."

"I don't suppose he can do that test right now?" I ask. "Get it all over with at once."

"Unfortunately not." Calliope shakes her head. "But never fear. The third test is not as physically demanding as the first two."

She swims off, making more notes as she goes.

"Well, that's a reassurance," I mutter.

"No worries," Quince says. "After those first two tests, anything else they throw at me has to be cake."

"Lily?" Daddy floats into my line of sight, reminding me that I have other obligations here tonight.

"Right," I say. Then, to Quince: "Why don't you go get some rest and something to eat? I have to talk with Daddy about my meeting with King Zostero."

Quince gives me a questioning look, but when I shake my head, he smiles. "Okay. Come find me when you're done?"

"Definitely."

I watch as Quince heads toward the palace, and the royal kitchen. Laver is going to have a heart attack.

"Let's talk in my office," Daddy says.

"Yes," I say. "Let's."

18

"**W**hat are we going to do?" I ask Daddy after I tell him what I learned from King Zostero. "He's not the only one planning sabotage attacks against humans. We don't even know what other kingdoms are involved. It could be *all* of them, for all we know."

"That is unlikely," he says. "But you are correct that this is far more unsettling than we imagined. Lily, I am so sorry I doubted you."

"I know you are, Daddy."

"If I could go back—"

"But you can't. And now we have an even bigger problem. How do we stop them?" I ask. "If this week's oil rig accident was just the first of many, things are only going to get worse."

"Honestly, Lily," he says, his shoulders drooping a bit, "I am not yet sure how to approach this. While I do not agree with their methods, I understand their motivations. It is hard to reason with the righteous."

Daddy starts shuffling papers on his desk, and I can tell he's at a loss. We don't have time to be at a loss. Human lives are at stake.

"Well, we have to come up with something," I insist. "We can't just sit by while they start these attacks. I won't."

"No, of course not. You and I will meet with my advisers, for as long as it takes, and we will come up with a plan. Mangrove," he calls out to his secretary.

"Yes, your highness," the eager-to-serve merman says as he swims into the office.

"Please ask Graysby and Grouper to come in for a meeting. We have important matters to discuss."

"Yes, sir."

"And please find Peri, too," I add. "She's my adviser, and I want her here."

"Yes, Princess." Mangrove disappears into the hall, and I can't help feeling like this isn't enough.

"I promise you, Lily," Daddy says, "we will figure out how to solve this."

"Pardon me, your highness," a royal guard says, peering into the room, "but Princess Waterlily has a visitor."

A visitor? Maybe Peri heard that I was home and is already here.

"Prince Tellin awaits you in the entry hall."

Okay, not Peri.

"Go," Daddy says. "We will begin the meeting without you."

I nod and swim out into the hall. As I follow the guard through the palace, I pass by Graysby and Grouper, Daddy's closest advisers, on their way to the royal office. Peri has a longer way to swim from her home outside the palace walls.

"What's wrong?" I ask Tellin as soon as I see him.

The guard who was escorting me disappears back into the palace. When Tellin turns to face me, there is pure panic in his eyes. I open my mind to the bond connecting us, and the panic I saw in his eyes assaults me tenfold.

"What?" I ask, darting to his side. "What happened?"

"Lily, I—" He swings his gaze around the space, as if checking for eavesdroppers. "Can we go speak somewhere private?"

Normally I would say that the palace staff knows better than to eavesdrop on their princess. But Tellin does not look like he's in the mood for verbal assurances.

"Of course."

I lead the way up to my room, where we won't be interrupted. As soon as we float inside, I say, "Tell me."

He wrings his hands and starts swimming in a circle. "My father . . . ," he begins, then trails off.

"Oh my gosh," I cry. "Is he okay? He's not—?"

"No," Tellin says with a pained laugh, "he's not dead. Lily, he's . . ."

The fear coursing through Tellin is pounding me.

"Please," I say, wanting this pain to lessen, "tell me."

Tellin draws in a quick breath and nods. "I think he's going mad, Lily," he says. "He . . ." He hesitates, shakes his head, and forces himself to continue. "He wants to start a war."

"What?" I gasp. "What are you talking about?"

"Since the council meeting, he has been consumed by anger," Tellin says. "I tried explaining that the other kings and queens only refused aid because they have terrible problems of their own. That we aren't alone, and that Acropora is not a failure because we suffer."

"Okay," I say, still trying to understand what he's saying. "How does that lead to *war*?"

"He said that if the other kingdoms wouldn't help, then he would *take* help from them." Tellin closes his eyes, and I'm pretty sure it's to hide their sparkling. "He has spent the past two weeks amassing an army to invade our neighbors, to plunder food and supplies."

"Your neighbors," I whisper. "You mean Queen Cypraea and her people?"

"Yes, Antillenes." When Tellin opens his eyes, they glitter bright orange. "And Thalassinia."

"What? Why?" I demand. "We have sent aid. We're doing everything we can to help."

"I know," Tellin snaps. "Don't you think I know that? Don't you think that's why I wanted to bond with you in the first place? Because your people already support us."

"I'm sorry," I say, not because I did anything wrong, but because I know Tellin is stressed beyond belief.

"I've tried talking to him," Tellin continues, almost as if I'm not there. "I yelled at him, argued with him, and begged him. He won't listen to reason."

There seems to be a lot of that going around lately. Desperate times lead to desperate acts. But war?

Though the history of the mer world is not without a few wars, there hasn't been one in my lifetime. There hasn't been one in the Western Atlantic for centuries.

But besides that, Thalassinia and Acropora have always been great allies. We are already sending what aid we can spare, food surpluses and medical supplies. We are welcoming Acroporan refugees with open arms. Thalassinian schoolchildren are even raising sea coins to help Acroporan children.

The idea that Acropora would *invade* Thalassinia is unfathomable.

"Tellin," I whisper, my brain in shock, "what are we going to do?"

"I don't know," he says. "My father won't listen to me. Or Lucina or his advisers or any of the nobles and ambassadors who have tried to change his mind. I have tried everything."

I feel bad for Tellin. He's trying so hard to do right by his kingdom, to help his people in this time of need and suffering. His father is not helping the situation.

"We'll have to tell my dad," I say, thinking of no better option.

190

"No! Lily, please," Tellin pleads. "That's why I came to you and not the king. I don't want my father's moment of madness to harm relations between our kingdoms. Or to ruin my father's reputation. For many decades, he has been an intelligent and respected ruler. If there is a way to stop this without your father finding out, I need to try that first."

"Then why come to me?" I ask. "What do you expect me to do?"

I'm already failing at my other missions—getting the mer kingdoms to work together to solve the ocean's environmental problems, and now stopping the mer kingdoms from sabotaging human enterprises. I'm not really sure I can do anything to help.

"My father has always liked you, Lily," Tellin says. "He respects your father, but he genuinely *likes* you."

"So what if he likes me?" I say. "Tellin, I can't keep this a secret. If there is a threat to our kingdom—"

"Talk to him," Tellin interrupts. "Come to Acropora and have a conversation with my father."

"Tellin . . ."

"If you can't convince him to change his plans," Tellin says, "then I'll return with you and tell King Whelk myself. Just please give him one chance."

How do I know what is the right thing to do? Keep this from Daddy, and maybe risk my kingdom's safety? Or tell him, and risk our relationship with Acropora?

Tellin's methods haven't always been well thought out in

the past. He did, after all, try to *force* me to bond with him. We got past that as soon as he finally told me what was going on. Then I bonded with him willingly.

It's a sign of progress that he's talking about the situation and not trying to make something happen through force or coercion.

But I have a responsibility to my people and their safety. I need to decide if it's worth the risk. Daddy is always telling me to lead first with my heart. Aunt Rachel is always telling me to trust my gut. I close my eyes and listen to my instinct.

King Gadus has always been kind to me. As a child, he used to slip me treats when Daddy wasn't looking. And even though he and Daddy eventually had a falling-out—over me and Tellin, it turns out—they were always friends.

And Thalassinia has always considered Acropora her closest ally. I can't throw that away without even *trying* to fix things.

"Okay," I say. "Let me tell Quince I'm leaving and give Daddy some excuse for skipping out. I'll meet you outside the palace gate in twenty minutes."

"Thank you, Lily," Tellin says, and I can sense his gratitude.

"It's just a conversation," I say. "And if it doesn't work—"

"We'll turn around and swim right back."

I nod. Tellin slips out the front door, and I head back to Daddy's office, to try to explain why I'm leaving before the meeting to discuss the problem I was so desperate to solve just minutes ago. I hope he never has to know.

Swimming over Acropora on our way to the palace, I can see things have changed. Many of their once-flourishing coral reefs are pale and lifeless. Their structures look tattered around the edges and in need of some routine maintenance. And their streets and plazas, which I remember always bustling with merfolk, are practically empty.

I know Tellin said his people were seeking better lives on land and in other kingdoms, but hearing and seeing the truth are two different things.

"Tellin, I . . ." I'm not sure what to say. "I'm sorry your kingdom is dying?" "Wish I could help?"

I'm trying, but I don't think that's what he wants to hear.

"I know," he says, swimming faster, like he's embarrassed by the state of his world. "Let's just get to my father and get this over with."

I force the tears from my eyes, knowing Tellin won't appreciate the sympathy. Right now, being here with him and trying to talk his father out of his crazy plan is enough.

Inside, the palace looks even more run-down than the rest of the city. It's like the king diverted funds from his own household to help his people first. I have to admire that.

"Father," Tellin calls out as we reach the royal chamber.

"What?" the old man's voice barks from within.

"I have Princess Waterlily with me." Tellin gives me a

hopeful look. "She wants to speak with you."

"Waterlily, eh?" he grumbles. "Well what are you waiting outside for?" he says. "Bring the guppy in."

I remember visiting the palace as a girl, being awed by the royal chamber. Even compared to Thalassinian standards, it had been impressive. In American colonial times, Acropora had been the center of a lot of pirating activity. That, in turn, led to a lot of pirate loot winding up within their borders.

A lot of times, the reason a pirate couldn't find his hidden booty—even with an X-marks-the-spot treasure map—was because some crafty Acroporan merperson had snuck up on land, dug it up, and claimed it as his own.

The royal chamber had been decorated with priceless gems and pieces of eight and other precious human treasures.

As I swim inside now, I'm shocked to see the walls and ceiling stripped bare. All the wealth that was on display is gone, leaving a chipped surface.

The situation here must have been deteriorating for years. Decades, even. They must have gradually stripped the valuable decorations to boost the treasury, to pay royal employees, and to buy goods from other kingdoms. Their backup reserves are all gone now.

At my gasp, Tellin cuts me a warning look.

I nod. He doesn't want me putting his father on the defensive about the state of the chamber. I draw my gaze away from the condition of the room and instead focus on the king himself. Seated in his throne, surrounded by several guards and what look like advisers, he sends them all away.

King Gadus looks like a shell of his former self, even worse than when I saw him at the council meeting. His skin is pale—not fair-skin pale, like mine, but ghostly pale with a grayish tint. There are dark bags under his eyes, and he is hunkered over in the throne, like a merman far older than I know he is.

It's heartbreaking.

"I can guess why you're here," he says to me, throwing his son an angry glare. "You can't talk me out of it."

"Your highness," I say, swimming closer. "You can't think—"

"Call me Gadus, girl," he barks. "We've known each other long enough."

"Gadus," I say, beginning again, "you can't think that this is the way to fix things."

"I witnessed your first attempt to *fix things* at that absurd council meeting. I'm an old merman," he says. "My kingdom is dying, and so am I. There aren't many choices left."

"This is not the right one," I insist. "Tellin and I are working on a plan to get help for your kingdom—for *all* the kingdoms."

"Working on a plan." He practically spits. "How long will that take? Weeks? Months? Years? Neither I nor Acropora have that kind of time."

"Then we'll make it happen faster," I say. "I will personally raid Thalassinia's stores and send everything we can spare. My father has already agreed to accept and provide for as many Acroporan refugees as we can support, and I'm sure we can get other kingdoms to agree to do the same."

Eventually, I add silently.

"It is not enough!" Gadus slams his fist against the arm of his throne.

"And you think starting a war will solve things?" I have to get through to him, and if he's worried about his kingdom, I have to make him see that this is the worst choice for his people.

"War comes at a great cost to a kingdom," I say. "It takes resources you don't have and risks the lives of the very people you're trying to save."

Gadus drops his head, and he's silent for so long, I start to think he's fallen asleep. I look at Tellin, but he's staring blankly at the ceiling.

I swim closer.

When Gadus lifts his head, I'm shocked to see his gray eyes sparkling. My heart aches for his pain.

"What other choice do I have, Lily?" he asks, and I get the feeling he is actually asking. He really wants my advice.

I wish I had an easy answer. I don't even have a certain answer, but I give him the only advice I have.

"Have patience," I say. "As much as you can find. And faith. You have to trust that your fellow merfolk will do what's right in the end."

Gadus snorts. "My fellow merfolk are idiots. They think breaking oil rigs and sinking ships is going to solve the ocean's problems. How can I expect them to help me when they're too dumb to help themselves?"

"You know about the sabotage efforts?" I ask.

"Of course," he grumbles. "That damn fool clownfish Dumontia came calling at my door, asking Acropora to join the cause. Threw her out on her ear, I did."

"Dumontia?" The queen of Glacialis. "She's behind it?"

Gadus nods, and I kick forward to plant a kiss on his wrinkled cheek. This is exactly what I needed to know. If I know who's behind the sabotage, then maybe I can talk her out of her plan.

"Promise me you won't start a war," I say, "and I think I know how to turn things around."

Gadus shakes his head sadly. "You're right," he replies. "We don't have the resources to feed our staff, let alone an army."

"I promise you, Gadus," I say, "I will find a way to get you more help."

"I hope so," he says. "My kingdom is fast running out of options."

"Come on, Tellin," I shout, pushing away from the throne and grabbing him by the wrist. "We have to get back to Thalassinia. We have a long journey to prepare for."

"Where are we going?" he asks.

"To the arctic," I reply. "We have to talk to a queen."

19

F irst thing Monday morning, I see Quince off with a pair of royal guards to swim him home. Daddy and his advisers—and Peri, who came for the meeting and stuck it out to the end, even though I wasn't there—have agreed that a series of royal visits from the king himself will convince the other rulers that the sabotage plan is a big mistake. I doubt that's going to help, but they clear his schedule, and he and his advisers will leave for Marbella Nova shortly after Tellin and I leave.

Maybe a kingly presence will make a difference, but I'm not betting on it. I'm starting at the top.

When I told Daddy my plan, he wanted to delay his first visit and escort me to Glacialis. After some arguing and insisting and giving him the same argument I gave before my confrontation with King Zostero, he relents. He understands this is my mission, and I want to do it on my own, without Daddy's weight behind me—if I can.

So, once Quince is safely away and Tellin, Peri, and I have a dozen guards to escort us, Daddy uses his trident to whip up a powerful enough current to get us to Glacialis in record time.

"The return current will begin about two hours after your expected arrival time," he tells me.

"That should be long enough," I say. "Either she'll see reason by then, or she'll have kicked us out."

Daddy nods. "Be careful, daughter. And good luck."

"Thanks," I say, giving him a quick hug before swimming back to join my group. "We'll need it."

We leave the palace, swimming east, where we run into the enhanced current. Usually Daddy's current boost is at the fast end of normal for the given waters, but I doubt the Gulf Stream has ever flowed this quickly before. I give Peri a look that says, "Here goes nothing," and we move into the fast-flowing water. Tellin and the school of guards swim in after us.

Staying streamlined, the flow speeds us north, through the kingdom of Trigonum, into Nephropida and then Rosmarus. Every mile brings us into cooler and cooler temperatures. Even though it's practically summer, the water around us is freezing cold. Everyone in our group uses mer powers to warm the sea around us so we are traveling in a bubble of lukewarm water.

Finally, as the current takes us through the Strait of Belle

Isle, we emerge in the southernmost tip of Glacialis.

The water up here is different. Not just colder, although it definitely is that, but it *feels* different. It looks different. Crisper blues and denser liquid. And whether because of its geography or the melting ice caps Dumontia claims are desalinating their waters, the salt content is far lower than in Thalassinia.

"The palace is just on the other side of that ice wall," Peri says.

She has really done her research.

I nod and follow her direction, swimming toward the vertical sheet of ice and then around it. On the other side I see a palace that looks like something out of a fairy tale.

The entire structure is pure white, so white the glacial blues of the world around it reflect off its surfaces. I count at least a dozen spires, sharp angular things thrusting up toward the surface like icy stalagmites.

"It looks completely out of sync with the environment," I say. "Aren't they worried about discovery?"

"Not up here," Peri says. "Not too many humans diving in these frigid waters."

"Besides," Tellin adds, "their shape is not *so* unusual."

I follow the direction he's pointing and see a similar-looking formation a few hundred yards away. Only that one looks completely natural and organic.

"Oh, wow," I say as we approach the main entrance.

A pair of merfolk swim by, one a mermaid with a tail the

color of glaciers. Pale icy aqua with touches of pale turquoise and sky blue. Her hair is such a pale blond, it looks almost as white as the icy palace.

The other, a merman, has a tail that is dark brown, almost black. Matching dark-brown hair flows long past his shoulders, and with a brown fur jacket on, he could easily pass for a seal or a walrus if he had to.

I never really thought about it, but I suppose over time merpeople naturally evolved to match the colors and textures of the world around them. My lime-green-and-gold scales fit in perfectly with the brightly colored fish and sea life in my kingdom's ecosystem. Up here, blending in with the ice or masquerading as an arctic mammal would definitely be an advantage.

To enter the palace, we swim through what feels like a curtain of ice cubes. Shards of ice hang down in strings, and the Glacialine guards pull them aside to let us in.

"I shall tell the queen of your arrival," one of her guards says.

He leaves, and the remaining guard—a mermaid not much older than me with gray-and-white hair—stares openly at us. Her pale-gray gaze sweeps over my brightly colored tailfin and then Tellin's. And then those of Peri and the guards.

"They're . . . beautiful," she says, the warmth of her breath clouding in the icy water.

"Thank you," I say, blushing. I gesture at her tailfin,

varying shades of gray from dark steel to nearly silver. "I think your scales are beautiful, too."

"Princess Waterlily, how nice of you to visit."

I look up at the sound of Dumontia's voice. She floats into the room like the queen that she is, pale silver hair floating behind her like a floe of ice. Two attendants, a pair I recognize from the council meeting, flank her. Her posture—rigid spine, hands relaxed at her sides, and chin elevated—tells me everything I need to know about her. She is powerful, she knows it, and she wants me to know it too.

Well, I'm not scared. Not anymore.

"This is not a social call, your highness," I say, bowing slightly and hoping that the sign of deference will put her in a more agreeable mood.

"No, I thought not," she says. "Come to make another plea for help for the poor dying kingdom?"

The false pity in her voice is intended to taunt Tellin, and it works.

He starts forward, and I throw out an arm to stop him. I nod at two of my guards, who swim to his side and, each taking one arm, pull him back next to Peri.

Yes, her snide comment was uncalled for, but his emotional reaction is just what she wants. It won't make this go any easier.

She reminds me of Brody's ex-girlfriend, Courtney. When I was crushing on Brody, she used to say mean, terrible things about me. And I just let her. Now that Doe is with Brody, Courtney tried her tactics again. Only Doe stood up to her, and Courtney backed down.

I hope that works with Dumontia.

"No, I haven't," I say, straightening my spine and trying to float a little higher. I could use the advantage. "I'm here to—" I debate using the word "tell," but I think she'll react badly. "*Ask* you to stop the acts of sabotage you have planned against humans."

"Oh, you are, are you?" She laughs, weakly, like she pities me. "I'm sorry you came all this way for me to say no, but . . . no."

"Dumontia," I blurt; then, when I see the look of insult on her face, I backtrack. "Your highness, this is not the way to solve the problems facing our kingdoms."

"No?" She floats closer, looming over me like an imperial icicle. "And what do you suggest *is* the solution? Band-Aids and care packages?"

"It's a whole lot better than your plan," Tellin snaps.

I throw him a silencing look and find Peri already shushing him.

Dumontia rolls her eyes at him. "I'll pass, thank you."

"You're not going to drive humans out of the ocean," I say, trying to make her see why her plan is doomed to fail. "You're going to confuse them and make them angry. And then, maybe, you'll make them curious enough to start investigating why all these accidents keep occurring in their offshore endeavors."

"Will I?" she replies with a mocking tone. "Oh, that would be such a shame."

"No," I say, building up steam, "it will be a disaster. If they start investigating, then it's only a matter of time before they——"

Dumontia lifts her eyebrows and gives me a casual shrug.

"You——" I can't believe she's implying what I *think* she's implying. "You *want* them to investigate. You *want* them to find one of us, to discover our greatest secret."

"No," she says, her voice dripping with sarcasm, "that's not at all what I want."

"Was that your plan all along?" I ask in disbelief. "To reveal our existence to mankind?"

The superior look on her face melts and she leans in, looking serious. Her voice is just loud enough for me to hear, but not anyone else in the room. "Can you think of a better way to make humans realize the gravity of the situation? They could care less if whales and polar bears and entire coral-reef habitats die out as a result of their disregard for the natural environment. But mermaids? Well, they might think twice about dumping pollution into our waters if they know we're here."

"Dumontia," I say, shaking my head. This time she doesn't show insult at my use of her name. "This is not the answer. This could be the worst mistake in our history."

"Or it could be our finest moment."

She doesn't understand. I've lived with humans for years.

I love a bunch of them, and I respect who and what they are. But I also know that things are never that easy. It wouldn't be, "Oh, look, here we are, let's have a party." Between scientific study and governmental intervention, revealing ourselves to the human world at large would likely be a disaster.

Clearly Dumontia doesn't see it that way. I wonder if the other kings and queens do.

"Does the rest of your coalition know about your ultimate plan?" I ask her. "Do they know you want to expose our existence, or did you bring them on board with the false promise of retribution and kicking humans out of our waters?"

I can read the answer on her face.

"I didn't think so." I swim closer still, so close only *she* can hear *me*. "You call off your plans, or I will expose you."

"So what?" she says. "They might not know this is my plan, but most of them will not care. Their thirst for revenge and freedom is stronger than their desire to keep our secret."

"You really believe that?" I ask. "I think you're wrong."

I think the other rulers of the Western Atlantic—and in the rest of the seven seas—would be horrified to learn that Dumontia's ultimate goal is to reveal our existence to humans. I think they'd do anything to stop her. And that might be just the thing I need to get them on my side.

"Try it," she dares me. "We shall see."

Then, with a dismissive swirl, she turns and swims out of the room.

"I knew this wouldn't work," Tellin says, shrugging free of the guards holding him. "No one listens to reason anymore. Maybe my father has the right idea after all."

"Don't be so melodramatic," Peri tells him.

"Besides," I say, "now that we know her secret, we can use it against her. I think I know how to stop the sabotaging. And, if that works, then it will pave the way to interkingdom cooperation and help for your people."

Tellin gives me a skeptical look.

"What plan is that?" Peri asks.

"You'll have to wait and see," I say with a smile. "Wait and see."

20

"Miss Molina?"

She looks up from her desk to where I'm standing in the door to her classroom. She smiles. "Yes, Lily?"

I walk to the brown plastic chair next to her desk and sit. "So I've been thinking about what you said, about wishing you had done something more to stop your friends who burned that boat."

"Yes," she says, her eyes sad. "I've been thinking about that since we talked, too."

"Well, I was wondering," I say, tugging at the hem of my skirt. "You knew they were doing something wrong, and now you know how badly things turned out, right?'

"Yes, exactly."

After my visit to Glacialis and learning what Dumontia's true purpose is in sabotaging human stuff, I thought I knew exactly what to do. I'd tell the other kings and queens what she was doing, and they would be just as outraged as I am.

But then, on the swim back and in the day since I got home, I started to worry. What if the other kings and queens *aren't* outraged? What if they think Dumontia's ends justify the means and that revealing ourselves to the human world is exactly what needs to be done?

Dumontia seems to think that's how they'll feel. If they were so quick to jump on the sabotage bandwagon, maybe they will think revelation is a good idea too.

Even if I think this is something we—as rulers and as mer people—might want to consider someday, I don't think this is the way to do it. Forcing the decision on all of mer-kind without discussion, without a vote. That's not right.

If that's the play, then maybe I have to do something more extreme to get the kings and queens to see reason.

I only have one chance to use Dumontia's secret plan to my advantage, one chance with the element of surprise. I need to use it well and wisely.

"If you had it to do over again," I say, getting to the point of my presence, "would you tell the police? I mean, would you turn them in to keep them from getting into bigger trouble?"

Her brown eyes get a faraway look. "In a heartbeat."

"That's what I thought," I say, sighing with relief. "Thank you."

"Lily," she says, "I know you don't want to talk about the specifics of what's going on." She smiles softly. "But if you are involved with people, or an organization, who are taking illegal action to achieve their goals, then maybe you should reconsider your involvement. You're still so young. I would hate to see you throw your future away because you got caught up in a cause."

I can't help but laugh. I appreciate her concern, misplaced as it is. No, Miss Molina doesn't know the whole truth about what's going on—she can't—but if she did, she'd see that I'm trying to prevent that very thing from happening.

"I promise you, Miss Molina," I say, bringing myself back to a serious place, "it's not like that at all."

"If you're certain?"

"I wish I could tell you all about it," I say, and am surprised that I actually mean it. If there was one human outside my circle of friends and family I would tell the truth to, then Miss Molina would be that person. She's smart and kind, and she cares about the oceans and the environment.

Even though I hope it doesn't happen the way Dumontia is trying to force, maybe one day I will be able to tell Miss Molina the truth about me.

"I understand, Lily," she says, patting my knee. "You are entitled to your secrets. But if they ever get to be too much to bear alone . . ."

I grin at her. "You'll be the first."

With a reassured certainty about my plan, I jump up and hurry out into the hall. I'm going to need everyone's help to make this happen, and I need to start tonight.

Doe and I are bent over stacks of kelpaper when Aunt Rachel gets home after work. She drops her bags on the bench by the door and walks over to the table.

"Another round of invitations?" she asks.

I nod. "Yes. I think I've figured out how to solve one of my problems. And if it goes well, it might solve them both."

"Well, if you two are working that hard," she says, "then it must be a pizza night. What kind would you girls like?"

"I don't care," I say. "Anything is fine."

Doe looks up from her careful calligraphy. "Pineapple and jalapeño, please."

"What?" I ask, making a face.

She shrugs. "It reminds me of Laver's special sweet-and-spicy roll."

I smile. I'd forgotten that was her favorite. "Okay, then I'll have that too."

While Aunt Rachel calls the pizza place, I slide another seal-stamped kelpaper sheet across the table to Doe.

"Thanks for helping me again," I say.

Doe shrugs, like it's whatever. "Brody had a family thing."

"I'm going to grab a quick shower," Aunt Rachel says, digging into her purse. "I'll leave the money here on the counter in case the pizza gets here before I'm done."

"Okay," I say, and then, when she's climbing the stairs, I return my attention to Doe. "Why do you always do that?"

She doesn't look up from her writing. "Do what?"

210

"Act like things are no big deal?" I stamp another sheet of kelpaper with squid ink. "It's okay to care, you know."

She is still and silent for several long seconds before finally answering. "Sometimes, when you care, it hurts more."

"But you *do* care," I insist. "I can tell. You just act like you don't."

"Well, I don't want to," she whispers. "I'd rather be care-free and aloof than wind up crying in my bed every night. Once was enough."

I take a shaky breath. I remember that one time all too well. She's talking about when her parents died. They were killed in a fishing-boat accident a few years ago, and I know Doe took it really hard. Who wouldn't? She didn't leave her room for weeks. It was months before she started attending palace events again. She was a different mergirl after that.

I always knew that was why she acted out, why she rebelled against Daddy and Uncle Portunus and anyone who tried to rein her in with rules and regulations.

I just never thought she was *trying* not to care. I thought she really didn't.

"Doe," I say quietly, "not caring won't protect you from pain. You can't stop yourself from—"

"I know, okay?" she snaps, accidentally scratching her quill across the half-finished invitation. "Damselfish." She sets the quill down and takes a deep breath. "I know I can't not care about stuff. About people. I screwed up that plan when I fell for Brody."

211

"So why?" I ask. "Why do you keep acting like that?"

"I don't know," she answers. "Habit, maybe? I've been pretending things didn't matter for so long, I guess it's hard to start accepting that they do."

She looks up at me, half a smile in place.

"I'm trying," she says.

"You're doing great," I insist. "It'll probably take some practice, is all."

"Well, I'm getting plenty of that." She gestures at the invitations in process, scattered over the table. "Between you and Brody and saving the mer world from itself *and* humans, I'm learning a lot about caring."

"Yeah, you—" I jerk back, realizing what she just said. "Wait, did you just say you cared about me?"

Her eyes widen, and she looks like she wants to deny it. Then, realizing she can't take it back, she sighs. "Yes. I suppose I did."

"Doe!" I squeal.

Jumping up from my chair, I rush around the table and pull her into a big hug.

"You love me," I blurt. "Admit it!"

She sighs again. Then, reluctantly, she lifts her arms and returns my hug. "Yes," she whispers, like she's afraid someone will overhear. "I love you."

I squeeze her tighter. "I love you too, cousin."

Lord love a lobster, if someone told me just a few weeks ago that Doe and I would be hugging and exchanging

I-love-yous over Aunt Rachel's kitchen table, I'd have told them to stop eating the fermented sea urchin.

Prithi meows from under the table.

"And we love you, Prithi," I say, scooping the cat up into my arms. She gives me a look that says "Die, half-human!" and then strains for Doe.

"Good news?" Aunt Rachel asks, rubbing a towel over her wet hair as she walks back into the kitchen.

Doe blushes as she takes the cat from me.

I don't want to push her too hard into the direction of publicly admitting to caring about anything, so I save her the embarrassment by saying, "Just . . . cousin stuff."

Aunt Rachel smiles, like that answer tells her everything she needs to know. She reads people really well, so she probably knows exactly what I mean.

"You girls almost done?" she asks. "The pizza should be here any—"

The doorbell rings.

"Ah, there it is." Aunt Rachel grabs the money off the counter.

"We're almost done," I say. "Just a couple more."

I reach for the green kelpaper and start on the two personal messages I want to send.

"Finish up and meet me in the living room," she says. "We can watch TV while we gorge."

Doe goes back to writing the text of the invitation. I compose my letters, still amazed at the change in Doe recently.

Part of it, I know, is her growing up. But another part of it is her feelings for Brody. Loving him—and getting over her hate for humans—is making her a better mergirl.

"I never thought I'd say this," I say, "but I'm really glad you kissed Brody."

She looks up and scowls at me, like maybe I'm going nuts. Maybe I am.

"I'm just getting sentimental in my old age," I tell her. "Watch out, because soon I'll be crying in my cereal every morning. And now that you've started caring about things, you're next."

The horrified look on her face is a joke. Mostly. But I know I'm right. Because once you start caring about something, it gets harder and harder to stop.

21

*T*he stench of chlorine in the air makes me choke a little as I emerge from the locker room. They must have treated the pool really recently.

I shake off the discomfort. A little allergic reaction is a small price to pay if my plan works.

"You're sure you want to do this?" Brody asks. He waves the video camera at me.

"Yes," I say, feeling more certain than maybe I should.

Shannen juggles the pieces of poster board that contain the words of the speech we wrote together.

I tug the beach towel tighter around my chest. I feel like this is the right thing to do, but it goes against every secrecy instinct I've been taught since birth.

Of course, that's what I'm counting on. That I'm not the only one who will feel this way, that every other mer king and queen—except Dumontia, apparently—has the same instinct.

"You're sure you don't want me in the shot too?" Doe asks.

"No," I say. "You're living on land now. I don't want you exposed if this all goes wrong. Besides . . ." I turn to the mergirls on either side of me. "I've got all the help I need."

Peri nods, her chestnut hair falling in silken waves over her shoulders. She tends to keep to the oceans, so I'm really glad she came.

"We're glad we can help, Princess," Astria says.

"Glad," Piper echoes.

Venus gives me a thumbs-up.

I smile at them, amazed that Astria actually came through on her promise to help. I guess she realized that the environmental problems facing the mer world are serious enough for her to set aside her childish behavior. Change is definitely in the water lately, and I'll take what I can get.

I laugh a little too, because Piper and Venus have also dyed the ends of their hair. Piper's is bubble-gum pink while Venus's is bright purple. Guess I've started a trend.

Doe goes to sit with Quince in the bleachers overlooking the pool. Luckily, Coach Hill gave Brody keys to the natatorium so he could work in a few extra practices. That means we were able to get inside late at night, when no one else is here.

I reach under the beach towel and push down my skirt,

leaving me in a tank top and finkini bottom behind the terry-cloth wrap. My legs shake as I bend down to pick up my skirt and throw it out of the shot.

"Okay, Lil," Brody says, punching buttons on the video camera. "I'm close in on you. Ready whenever you are."

Shannen holds up the cue cards.

I take a deep breath, force my hands to my sides, and smile.

The red light comes on. The camera is rolling.

"Hi, I'm Lily Sanderson," I say to the lens, my voice quivering with nerves. "I am a student at Seaview High School in Seaview, Florida. And my friends and I have a secret."

Shannen flips to the next card.

Brody pushes a button, and I hear the whir of the zoom as he backs out to get all of me in the shot. I reach up and grab the towel, pulling it away and revealing my swim-ready outfit underneath. And farther still to get the other girls.

Then, with a nod at Brody to make sure he's ready, I turn and dive into the pool. Beside me, Peri and the terrible trio—I guess I'll have to give them a new nickname now—do the same. I transfigure as I arc through the air, and my finkini turns into a full-on tailfin. As I slip into the water, eyes closed and breath held so I don't get too much chlorine exposure, I make sure to give my tailfin an extra wave for the camera.

I loop around underwater, turning back to the pool's edge, and pop up right at the wall. Bracing my crossed arms on the concrete edge, I kick gently below water to keep me level enough to meet the camera lens.

The other girls pop up next to me. We must make quite a picture.

Shannen holds up the next part of the speech.

"Yes," I say, ignoring the sting of chlorine on my skin, "I am a mermaid."

With one extrapowerful kick, I launch myself up onto the edge of the pool. Sitting on one hip, still flanked by my girls in the water, I arrange my tailfin so it spreads out next to me.

"And we aren't the only ones," I say, hurrying to the rest of my speech so the girls can get out of the pool and we can go rinse off the chlorinated water.

Shannen scrambles to keep up with my pace.

"There are hundreds of thousands of merfolk in the world's waters. We have lived in secret for millennia, but now"—I give the camera an extrabrilliant smile—"our secret is out. You might be wondering *why* I've decided to reveal my people's existence. It wasn't an easy decision. But when I learned that some merfolk, motivated by the environmental changes affecting our oceans, wanted to exact revenge by sabotaging human ships, drilling platforms, and tourist destinations . . . well, I couldn't just sit by and do nothing. I hope that by telling you, mankind, about our existence, lives will be saved."

Shannen flips to the final card.

I ignore it.

My smile wavers, and I go off script. "I also hope that together we will be able to find solutions to the changes affecting both of our worlds. We all need to work together."

I hold my look at the camera until Brody says, "Cut."

The four girls in the pool pop out onto the deck, shedding their tailfins in the process.

I shiver as I transfigure back into legs and a finkini. My exposure to the heavily chlorinated water was brief, but I can still see my skin turning red from the toxic contact. The other girls must be far worse.

"Let's go rinse off," I say to them. "We'll be right back."

As we stand under the streaming water, I only hope I'm doing the right thing. At least I'm not doing it alone.

"Thank you," I say to the girls. "For swimming all this way and agreeing to be a part of this crazy plan."

"The changing oceans affect us too," Astria says.

Venus adds, "We're glad to help in any way we can."

Piper seems to be enjoying the scalding-hot water too much to parrot her friends.

Peri gives me a look that says, "Did I wake up in Opposite World?"

I shrug and smile. I'm not going to question this change for the better.

When we return to the pool area, Quince and Doe are huddled around the camera as Brody shows them the video.

"Did it turn out okay?" I ask.

Brody says, "Yeah, great."

Doe gives me a sad look. "You're sure this is going to work?"

"Sure?" I repeat. "No. But I think it will."

"I wish I could be there to see their faces," she says. "I bet Uncle Whelk has a coronary."

"I hope not." I wring out my dripping hair into the pool. "It'll be better if you're not around."

"I know," she says.

"I'll tell you all about it," I promise.

"If you don't need us anymore, Princess," Astria says, "then we should be getting home."

"No, you've done more than enough," I reply.

Maybe I didn't really *need* them to be part of the video, but it made me feel better to do this with backup. And hopefully it will have a lot more impact with several of us revealing our mer selves at once.

"I'll get going too," Peri says. "We can swim home together."

I watch in awe as Peri and the . . . not-so-terrible trio walk to the door. Together.

"Good luck," Peri calls out as they head into the night. "Let me know how it goes."

"Thank you," I shout after her. "I will."

I sigh and turn back to Doe, Brody, and Quince.

"You're all ready for your meeting, then?" Quince asks.

"I guess so."

"So how about we take a quick ride down the coast?" he suggests. "It'll clear your head."

"That," I say, stepping close and wrapping my arms around his neck, "is a spectacular idea."

"I'll get the video processed and ready to go," Brody says. "I'll leave it on a jump drive for you."

"Thanks, Brody," I say. "It means a lot."

"No problem," he says with that curving smile that used to make me swoon.

Doe walks to his side and slips an arm around his waist.

"Everything will go great," she says. "I just know it."

"Thanks," I say, not sure how to handle her compliment.

"Besides," she says with a little of that old Doe attitude, "if you screw up, we can always run away to Antillenes. I hear they have no extradition to other kingdoms."

I laugh as I let Quince lead me out into the night. He climbs onto his bike and I take the spot behind him. For a little while, I can forget about all the pressures of tomorrow's council meeting. For tonight, it can just be about me and Quince.

22

$\mathcal{T}$he open-air cruise up the coast and back refreshes me almost as much as a saltwater bath. Maybe it's the salty sea air, or maybe it's spending an hour with my arms tight around Quince's waist. Either way, I feel ready to take on the mer world.

When we pull into the driveway between our houses, I see the lights are on in my kitchen. It's pretty late and Aunt Rachel knew I would be out with Quince, so I wonder why she's up.

"I'll walk you in," Quince says, stomping down the kick-stand on his bike.

We walk inside and find that Aunt Rachel isn't the one up waiting for me.

"Daddy?" I ask, surprised to see him sitting at the kitchen table. I can almost count on one hand the number of times he's been in this house since I came to live here. Most of

222

them in the past few weeks. "And Calliope? What are you two doing here?"

"Let me guess," Quince says, shutting the door behind us. "Time for test number three?"

Calliope gives me a sympathetic look.

"Not exactly," Daddy says.

"What?" I say. When neither of them explains, I repeat with a slightly higher tone, "What?"

"You couldn't have known," Calliope says.

Daddy shakes his head. "It was a tiny mistake."

"What do you mean?" I look nervously from one to the other.

"In the first test," Calliope explains, her expression sad, disappointed maybe, "you gave Quince directions to Thalassinia?"

"Yeah," I say. "So?"

"So," she says, her eyes softening, "that was technically against the rules of the trial."

"Against the rules?" I echo, my voice barely a whisper.

"It didn't help me," Quince says, stepping to my side. "I already knew how to get there."

"That," Daddy says with a frown, "is beside the matter."

"What does this mean?" I ask.

"Do I have to repeat the first test?" Quince asks. "Because I'll do it if I have to."

"I'm afraid that isn't an option," Daddy says.

He drops his gaze to the table, and my heart plummets.

If Daddy can't even look me in the eye, then this must be bad. Really bad.

"Technically, that counts as a forfeit," Calliope says. "You have failed the trial."

"No way," Quince roars.

I shout, "That's not fair."

Daddy keeps his face passive. "I know it isn't. But it is the rule."

My heart is pounding in my chest like it wants to explode. I can feel the tears pooling in my eyes. I step close against Quince's side, needing to feel him. He wraps his arm around my shoulder and tugs me closer.

"So . . . what?" Quince asks. "Now I'm stuck forever on land and Lily has to return to the sea? That's stupid."

Daddy and Calliope exchange an uncertain look.

"The situation is not quite so dire," she says, unrolling a kelpaper scroll on the table. "Because you failed on a technicality, rather than an outright inability to complete the test, there are contingency consequences."

I don't like the way she says that. Contingency consequences don't sound like we get to go for cookies and sushi instead.

"What's that?" I ask, afraid of the answer.

"The choice will be Quince's," she says, turning away from me and focusing on him. "There is a way for Lily to maintain her freedom, to be able to divide her time between land and sea."

My stomach drops.

"Okay," Quince says. "What's that?"

Calliope takes a deep breath before saying, "You have to give her up."

"What?" I cry. "No!"

"What does that mean?" Quince asks, his voice far more level than it should be. His arm tightens around my shoulder.

"You can't seriously consider this," I say, but everyone in the room is ignoring me.

"If you agree to never see her again," Calliope says, "right now, tonight, then she will be able to live in both worlds."

"And if I don't?"

"Then she returns to the water," Calliope says. "Forever."

"Done," Quince says.

"No," I shout. "This is ridiculous. You can't just say 'done' and end what's between us."

I pull out of his grasp and smack him on the shoulder. My tears overflow and spill down my cheeks when I see the pained look on Quince's face. This can't be happening, not after everything we've been through. Not after everything we've already overcome.

"Tell me there's another option, Lily," he says to me. "If I don't, you're back in the sea and I'm on land and we're over anyway."

"I . . ." Shaking my head, I can't believe this is happening. "No. I don't accept this." I look at Daddy. "There has to be another way."

He looks at Calliope, who is studying the kelpaper scroll again. "Well, there is one other option. . . ."

"What is it?" I blurt. "We'll take it."

"You don't even know what it is," Quince says, trying to sound all reasonable.

I glare at him. "If it means we'll get to be together, then I don't care what it is."

"You'll have to give up land, Lily," Daddy says. "If you agree to never step foot above the surface again, then Quince will be free to come and go in the sea. You can still be together."

"Yes, okay," I say without hesitation. "I choose that."

Quince grabs me by the elbow. "Can we talk about this for a second? Outside?"

Without waiting for my response, he leads me out the kitchen door. And I let him. As far as I'm concerned, though, there's nothing to discuss.

He steps down to ground level and turns around, forcing me to stay on the step above him.

"What is there to talk about?" I ask. "This is a no-brainer."

"I—"

"No," I say when he starts to argue. "You listen to me. I'm the reason we're in this situation in the first place. I'm the one who severed our bond, even though my feelings for you were growing. I'm the one who bonded to Tellin when I knew I loved you."

"Lily—"

"I know you like to be all tough and manly and you think you're the only one who should make sacrifices for us." I swipe at the tears on my cheeks. "But I'm a big mergirl. I know what I want, and I want to be with you."

Quince presses his hand over my mouth. "If you would let me get a word in, princess," he says, grinning like a little boy, "I love you. And I know this is a sacrifice for you because you love living on land almost as much as you love being in the water. But if this is your choice, I respect it and I'm honored by it."

"I . . . ," I say, breaking into a grin of my own. "Oh."

Leaning down, I press my lips against Quince's and feel the connection, the heat of his mouth on mine. I sigh. There isn't much I wouldn't sacrifice to be able to do this whenever I want.

"See," he says, tilting his chin away so our foreheads are still touching, "if you stop to listen every once in a while, you might hear good things."

I am just about to throw back some witty reply when I hear clapping. Twisting around, I see Daddy and Calliope standing in the still-open door.

"Hey," I say. "We're trying to have a private moment here."

"So we heard," Calliope says. The smile on her face is bigger than I've ever seen, bigger even than when she first realized that Quince loved me.

"We could not delay our congratulations," Daddy says.

227

"We have already put you through enough."

"Congratulations?" I repeat. "What are you talking about?"

"We're talking about the third test," Calliope says.

"I thought there was no third test."

Calliope shrugs innocently. "This *was* the third test."

"This?" I shake my head, trying to get the silt to settle in my mind. When it does, my jaw drops. Oh no, I cannot believe they pulled this on us. And I *cannot* believe I fell for it. "Are you kidding me?"

"I told you the third test would be emotional," she says with a sappy grin. "What I didn't tell you was that it would test both of you."

"You both had to make a difficult emotional decision," Daddy says. "You both had to be willing to sacrifice." He beams. "And you were."

My mind roars at the thought of what they just put us through. The emotional turmoil of thinking that I would lose Quince forever, that he would give me up so I could keep my freedom, and then that I would give up my freedom so I could keep him, was pure torture. Without stopping to think, I punch Daddy in the arm.

"That wasn't nice," I chide.

"I know," he says, rubbing at his shoulder. "But it was the requirement of the test."

Fine. I know Daddy wouldn't have put me and Quince through this if he didn't have to. And at the moment I guess

I'm just so relieved that the trial is over that I'm willing to forgive the game.

"Just promise me one thing," I say, stepping up so I'm closer to eye level with him. "No more tests."

"No," he says with a laugh. "No more tests."

"Or challenges," I say, wanting to clarify as much as possible. "Or ancient laws or long-forgotten rules or consequences or anything at all that will affect my relationship with Quince."

Daddy's humor fades, and his expression is all seriousness as he says, "No, none of the above."

"Well," Calliope interrupts, "there is the *duplex amoris*."

Daddy and I both turn to glare at her.

She blushes. "But that only comes into effect if you fall in love with twins from the Southern Hemisphere."

I glare harder.

"Look at the time," she says. "Seems like my work here is done. I'll sign off on the challenge as soon as I get back to the palace." She twists past me and Quince and grabs her bike from where it's leaning against the house. She climbs onto the seat and calls out, "Good-bye," as she pedals down the driveway. "Love the blue hair."

"I swear," I say when she disappears around the corner, "that woman is out to make my life difficult."

From behind, Quince slips his arms around my waist. He pulls me back down a step, and I lean into his body.

"She means well," Daddy says. "I really am sorry that you

had to go through that. If there had been any way around the law—"

"I know, I know," I say. I place my hands on Quince's arms. "As long as we're together at the end of the day, that's all that matters."

Daddy nods. "Well, I'll leave you two, then."

"I'll see you tomorrow night," I say. "At the council meeting."

"Tomorrow night."

When Daddy is gone and Quince and I are alone, he laughs. "I don't think I'll ever understand your mer-world ways," he says.

I turn in the circle of his arms. "Luckily, you'll have a whole lifetime to figure it out."

"Heaven help me." He rolls his eyes comically.

"Ha ha." I plant a quick kiss on his mouth. "Now get going. I need a good night's sleep, and I think I'm going to need like a three-hour bath to soak away all the stress in my bloodstream right now."

"You know where I'll be if you need me."

I smile. "Always."

$\mathcal{T}$he doorbell rings a few minutes before the meeting is scheduled to begin, and my heart starts racing. I smooth my hands over the knee-length gray skirt Aunt Rachel bought me when I started interviewing for jobs after my sixteenth birthday. That plan quickly fell apart because employers—even fast-food restaurants and souvenir shops—like to have a Social Security number for their potential employees.

But I kept the skirt for special occasions.

Today definitely qualifies as a special occasion.

I cross the living room, my black ballet flats scuffing across the floor. I feel like I'm about to be executed.

If things go wrong, maybe I will be.

I wish I didn't have to face them alone. Aunt Rachel's living room will be a tight squeeze with just me, Tellin, and the ten rulers. Which is part of the reason I asked them to leave their advisers and attendants in the surf. We don't have the space to accommodate their entourages.

As much as I want Doe or Peri or even the not-so-terrible trio at my side, I'd be all kinds of hypocritical if I didn't play by my own rules.

At the door I take one more second to tug at the hem of my short-sleeve cotton blouse. The pale blue isn't exactly Thalassinian royal colors, but it will have to do. I'm trying to project a mature and responsible image, and this is the closest thing I've got in my closet.

Taking one last deep breath for confidence—or extra oxygen to keep me from passing out—I paste a welcoming smile on my face and grab the handle.

"King Tiburo. Queen Sula." I spread my arms wide and gesture into the house. "Welcome to my home."

The rulers of Rosmarus and Nephropida, two of the most northern kingdoms in our region except for Glacialis, sport twin sour looks on their faces. I was expecting this kind of reaction. It's not every day—meaning never—that a council of kings and queens is called to a land-based location.

Daddy assured me it was possible, but he also warned me that the other kings and queens would be unhappy. Many of them haven't stepped out of the water in years. Some never have.

But this is all part of my plan. There are two main advantages to meeting on land, and one of them is that I will have what Quince calls the home court advantage. The kings and queens are coming onto my turf—even Daddy.

"Please," I say, leading Tiburo and Sula to the living room and pointing at the trays of grape juice and sushi set out around the room. "Help yourself to some refreshments."

They stand awkwardly, not taking me up on my offer. Their loss. Mushu makes the best sushi in Seaview.

The doorbell rings again, and I grab a spider roll on my way back.

I greet Queen Otaria of Marbella Nova, whose arrival is followed by Queen Cypraea of Antillenes, Queen Palmara of Costa Solara, and King Zostero. He gives me the darkest look of all.

Daddy arrives next with King Gadus, with Tellin at his side.

I'm relieved that so far everyone seems to have agreed to my request to come alone.

The other reason I want this meeting to be limited to only the ten kings and queens and me and Tellin is because I want as few witnesses to what I'm about to do as possible. Gossip—especially royal gossip—travels fast underwater.

If things go well, no one outside this room will ever know what I've done.

King Bostrych arrives, his rotund body looking out of place on spindly legs. He heads straight for the sashimi spread on the side table at the far end of the couch.

That leaves just one attendee missing. I'm so not surprised.

I weave through the crowd to Daddy's side.

"She's late," I whisper.

"She'll be here," he says. "She has no choice."

I give him a meaningful look. "We didn't exactly part on great terms."

"Let me rephrase," he says. "If she wants to keep other kingdoms on her side, she knows she must be present."

As if on cue, the front door flies open and Dumontia steps inside. Her long silver hair floats around her like she's walking into a fan. Two guards flank her, following her inside.

"Queen Dumontia," I say, forcing my biggest smile yet. "Thank you for coming."

Her smile is equally fake. "How could I refuse?"

She didn't refuse, but she did ignore my request that she come alone.

"Perhaps you missed the part of the invitation where I asked everyone to leave their attendants and advisers behind." I nod my head at her two guards. "Please send your escorts back to the beach."

"A silly request," she says.

When she starts to move into the room, I step into her path.

"It may be a silly request," I say, repeating the words Doe told me to use, "but it is a condition of the meeting. If you'd rather abdicate your vote . . ."

Dumontia scowls, angry that I've used council protocol against her, I'm sure. But she doesn't argue. Instead, she snaps her fingers, and the two guards retreat back the way they came.

"Let's get this ridiculous meeting over with," she says, sweeping past me. "I have important matters of state to attend."

"I don't see any reason to delay." I move to the center of the living room, in front of the TV, which is the only flat surface not covered with drinks and eats. "If everyone would please take a seat."

Between the couch and recliner and the chairs Doe, Aunt Rachel, and I dragged in from the kitchen and down from upstairs, there are enough seats for everyone. The kings and queens grumble a bit, but they all find places to sit, and suddenly all of their attention is on me.

I clasp my hands behind my back, squeezing tight to steady myself.

"Last time I called a council," I begin, "I was asking for pledges of aid for an ailing kingdom. Instead of receiving the support I expected from my fellow merfolk, I learned that Acropora is not the only kingdom suffering in the wake of ocean warming and other environmental changes."

There are several murmurs of agreement, but no one interrupts.

"I was shocked and intimidated by the sheer size of the situation, but with the help of some friends, I realized that if I broke the problem up into smaller pieces, and if our kingdoms worked together rather than fending for ourselves, we could avert catastrophe with a swell of momentum that is greater than the sum of our parts."

I take a breath. This is the point where I stopped when I told Daddy my plan. As far as he knows, I'm just trying to raise support for the interkingdom commission on environmental change.

That will come after this next part, assuming this next part goes right.

"Then I learned something unfathomable. Some of our kin had decided that taking revenge on humans through acts of sabotage would be the best way to protect our future."

I keep my gaze steady on Tellin so I don't accidentally single out any rulers. I don't want to put anyone on the defensive.

"Maybe it is," King Zostero argues anyway.

I give him a look. "I won't go into *why* I think this is not the answer right now—although I think that reason should be obvious—because I know something else that most of you don't. Queen Dumontia, the leader of this sabotage movement, has ulterior motives."

Some of the kings and queens shrug. Others, Daddy and Gadus included, turn to look at Dumontia.

"Her goal is not to get humans *out* of our oceans," I explain, "but to bring them *in*. She wants to taunt humans into investigating the source of the sabotage. Into ultimately discovering our existence."

Several gasps echo in the room.

"She wants to reveal our secret to the world," I finish, "by circumventing our oversight procedures."

"Why, Dumontia?" Daddy asks, his face wrinkled in confusion.

A couple of other rulers quietly echo Daddy's question.

Dumontia stands, taking center stage. "Why?" she repeats. "Because it is the only way. To reveal ourselves to humans is the only way to make them see the harm they do to the oceans. Learning that magical creatures such as ourselves live in the seas might finally make them understand that they cannot carelessly pollute and destroy our environment."

"That's madness," Daddy says. "You cannot know that will be the result."

"We cannot know it won't, either," Zostero argues.

"Ridiculous notion," Gadus grumbles.

Tellin pats him on the shoulder.

"Maybe she's right," Queen Sula says. "Maybe this is our best chance."

"Our best chance?" Queen Otaria argues. "Perhaps our best chance of becoming human science experiments."

"That would be a better fate than slowly going extinct as the oceans die around us."

"We're not going extinct."

"We will if things don't change."

The room erupts into arguments. Some of the rulers see Dumontia's plan for the craziness it is, while others think it's a plan worth considering. As the debate grows louder and less controlled, I turn around and flip on the TV. I drag my fingertip over the touchpad on the laptop Brody set up this morning, and I pull up the video we shot yesterday.

I click play, turn the volume to full, and then step out of the way.

My heart is racing, and I cross my fingers behind my back.

No one notices at first. They are yelling at each other, and their voices drown out my video.

Then Tellin, who is the only person in the room who knows what's going on, shakes his father's shoulder and points to the TV. The two queens Gadus had been arguing with follow his gaze, and all three fall silent as they watch me, Peri, and the not-so-terrible trio dive into the pool.

Gradually, the other kings and queens notice. By the time the video ends, all eyes in the room are glued to the small screen.

The video loops back to the beginning and starts again. Brody did a masterful job with the editing, making the whole thing look like a series of news broadcasts. The rulers watch in silence as I make my confession, transfigure mid-dive, and climb back out onto the deck.

When the clip reaches the end and loops back to the start again, I click pause.

"Is this what we want?" I ask, pointing at the frozen image of Brody sitting at a news desk with a headline on the green screen behind him that reads MERMAIDS ARE REAL! "Videos of mermaids and mermen showing on every channel in every country around the world? Because you know the news of our existence would not stay confined to our region of the ocean. We would be outing every merperson in every body of water on the planet."

Ten pairs of eyes stare, unblinking, at the screen. Only Tellin looks at me. He gives me an encouraging nod, and I continue.

"Because if this is what we want, I can do it without its costing a single human life." I hold up my cell phone. "My friend who helped me make this video is waiting for a message from me. All I have to do is send the word, and he'll email it to every newswire on the internet. They'll have it in broadcast-ready HD in Paris, Dubai, and Hong Kong before you've made it back to Seaview Beach."

Everyone looks too stunned to react, even Dumontia. She is staring at me like I'm some previously undiscovered species of poisonous blowfish.

For the first time since I got this crazy idea, I feel like it might actually work.

"Should I tell him to send it?" I hold up my phone, placing my finger over the send button.

Every single person in the room—every single one—simultaneously shouts, "No!"

"You're sure?" I ask, looking directly at Dumontia.

Her mouth moves like she's grinding her teeth. This is

the moment when I think she realizes that she's lost. She and I are playing a high-stakes game of political chess, and I just called checkmate.

"Don't," she says, so quietly I almost don't hear.

"What was that?" I need everyone to hear her say it.

"Don't send the video," she enunciates. "Don't reveal our secret."

I nod and put my phone away. I want to smile, but I think I'll save that for later.

I catch Daddy's gaze across the crowd, and I can tell he's a little bit irritated at me for this risky tactic. He's also proud. I have a feeling there's a lecture in my future, but for now I have to finish my business.

"So we're all agreed that revealing ourselves to humans is *not* the best idea ever?" Everyone nods—some more reluctantly than others. For those reluctant ones, I feel like I have to spell it out. "And if sabotaging human objects could draw their close attention to our world, then that's an equally bad idea?"

More nodding and agreement, and I finally feel relief.

I reach behind me and turn off the computer and the TV.

"Now, if sabotage is off the table as the answer to our problems," I say, heading into the part of my speech that might actually be productive, "then I think we also agree that we need to work together to find another solution. Now, let me tell you about my ideas."

As I start explaining the purpose and procedures of the

interkingdom commission on environmental change, about the streamlined disaster relief and the resource matrix, I can see pride in Daddy's eyes. King Gadus's, too. And through our connection, I can feel Tellin's relief that his kingdom might actually stand a chance.

Their pride and relief fill me with some of my own. My first act as crown princess took a little longer than anticipated, but the pieces are finally coming together. Crown Princess Waterlily is on a roll.

24

"*L*ily. Sanderson."

Principal Brown's voice booms out of the speakers and echoes across the Seaview High football stadium. The crowd of parents, siblings, teachers, and staff applauds.

On shaky legs, I get up from the folding chair—third seat in, eighth row back—and make my way down the grassy field to the temporary stage. I climb the three steps up onto the stage, cross to where Principal Brown stands in front of the microphone, and take his offered hand.

In his other hand is a scroll of paper, tied with a pretty blue ribbon. He guides me to face the camera and, as the flash pops in my eyes, he presses the scroll into my hand.

"Congratulations, Lily."

I smile and flee off the stage on the other side. When I get back down to the grass, I turn to face the crowd in the stands above the field. The seating is general admission, so my friends and family could be anywhere, but with Tellin in attendance I just follow the sense of the bond.

I zero in on their location and hold up the scroll, my hard-earned diploma.

Even across the field, I can hear them cheering, Daddy, Aunt Rachel, Doe, and Tellin. Quince's mom is up there, too. Even Peri made the trip back to watch me walk at graduation—sporting chestnut hair with vivid orange tips.

My other nearest and dearest are in the sea of students with me. Brody is somewhere very near the front, with Quince just a couple rows behind him. Shannen is at the very back, and we'll have to wait almost to the end to see her get her diploma. And honor cords. And perfect attendance award. And state scholarship certificate.

She has the longest graduation résumé of anyone in our class. And I'm so proud that she's my best human friend.

I'm proud of all of us, for sticking it out and making it through.

And as soon as the ceremony is over, Daddy and I have a special graduation surprise planned for Quince. After the last name is called, the crowd in the stands descends on the field of new graduates. Aunt Rachel takes a million pictures, and Quince's mom takes almost as many.

By the time they're done, the stage is cleared and most of the stadium is emptied. As our friends and family finally disperse, I order Quince into my car.

"Where are we going, princess?" he asks, lifting his

eyebrows suggestively. "You going to kidnap me and take me to your magical kingdom?"

I just smile and keep driving.

I make it to the beach without stalling out once. This is definitely an improvement, although I did lurch through a few intersections along the way.

When we get there, everyone is waiting for us. Well, everyone but Quince's mom—we're still trying to figure out how to tell her about the mer world. I pull into a parking spot at the far end of the lot.

Quince starts to climb out of the car, but I put my hand on his arm to stop him. I want this moment to be about us.

"So, after the council meeting, Daddy gave me some good news."

"What's that?" he asks. "Something about your inter-kingdom commission?"

"No," I say, smiling. "It's about you."

"Oh yeah?" He sounds equal parts intrigued and concerned. "Not another test?"

I twist around to face out the driver's window, pulling my hair to one side to reveal my neck.

"You know there are two parts to a mer mark," I say, picturing the green design at the base of my neck.

I feel the heat of Quince's fingertips an instant before he begins tracing the design. "The waves on the outside," he says, drawing a circle on my neck, "and the flower in the middle."

"Exactly." I let my hair fall back into place as I turn to face him. "The waves represent *aqua respire*. The ability to breathe water."

I reach up behind Quince's neck and touch the spot where I know he has his own circle of waves, marked in black on his tan skin.

Quince covers my hand with his.

"The flower," I say, knowing that tears—happy ones—are right on the verge of filling my eyes, "represents *aqua vide*."

"*Aqua vide*," Quince repeats. "What's that?"

"It literally means water life," I say. "It's what allows a merperson to transfigure between mer and terraped form. It's what grants them the magical powers of our people."

"Lily," Quince says, taking his hand off mine and laying it against my cheek, "what's this all about?"

I nod at the spot halfway down the beach where our small crowd is gathered.

"When we walk over there, Daddy is going to finish your mark," I say. The tears spill over as I look into Quince's Caribbean-blue eyes. "You're going to be a merman."

He blinks several times, and I can't decide if he's stunned or freaked or just confused. For the millionth time, I wish we still had the connection of the bond to answer these things for me. Then again, it's probably better if I have to learn how to figure these things out for myself.

"Only if you want to, of course," I say, not wanting him

to feel pressured into doing this if he's freaked. "I won't be hurt or anything, if you don't—"

"Are you kidding?" Quince blurts, finally breaking his silence. "What are we waiting for?"

He throws open the door and jumps out. He's halfway across the beach by the time I climb to my feet. He turns back and, gesturing me to hurry, shouts, "Come on! I want a tailfin."

I laugh and follow him across the sand. I hope the mer world is ready for a Quince with a tailfin. As I slip my hand into his, I know that I am. It's about time.